THE BIOTECHNOLOGY REVOLUTION

# CLONING

EDITED BY KARA ROGERS

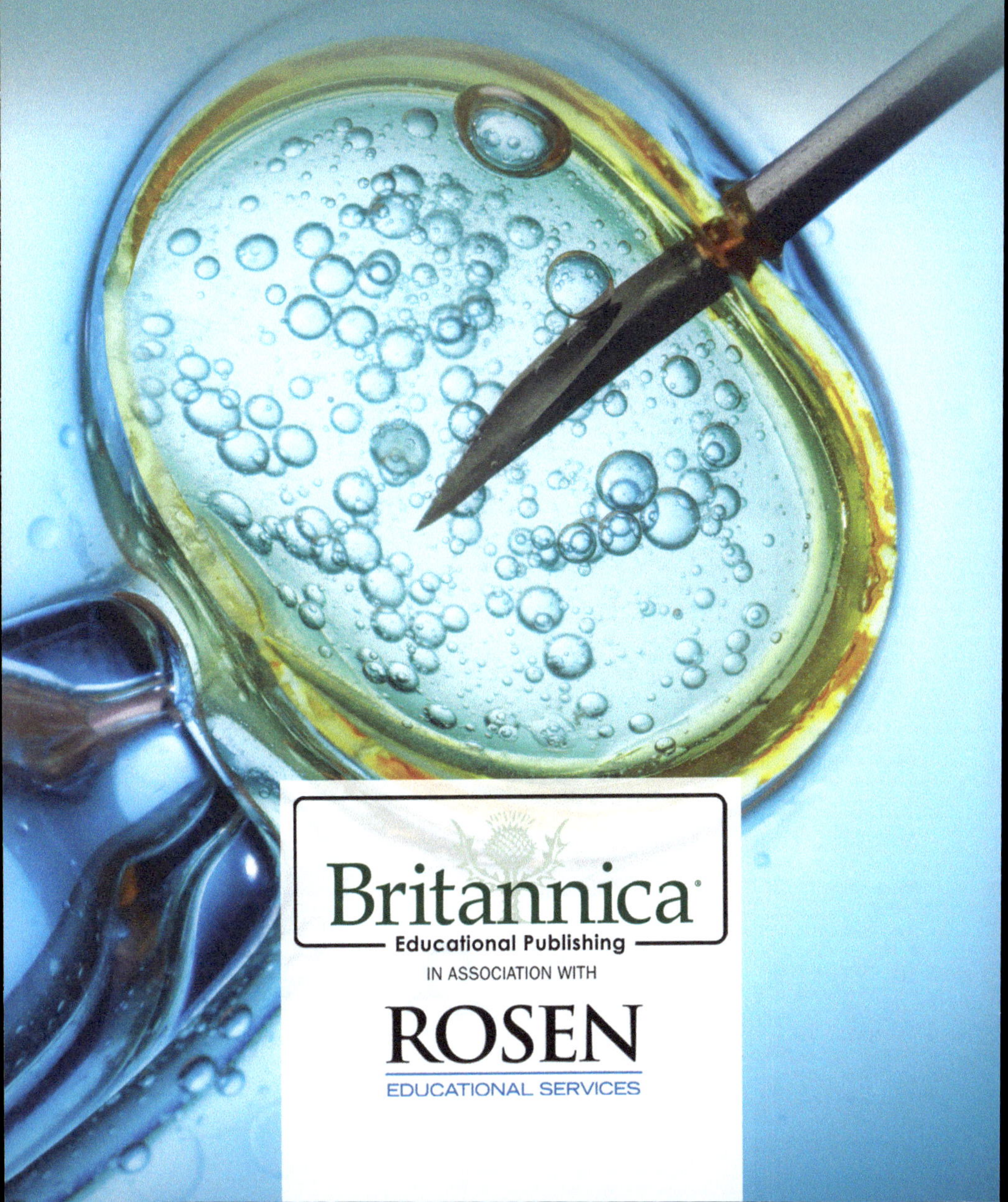

Britannica Educational Publishing
IN ASSOCIATION WITH
ROSEN
EDUCATIONAL SERVICES

Published in 2016 by Britannica Educational Publishing (a trademark of Encyclopædia Britannica, Inc.) in association with The Rosen Publishing Group, Inc.
29 East 21st Street, New York, NY 10010



Distributed exclusively by Rosen Publishing.
To see additional Britannica Educational Publishing titles, go to rosenpublishing.com.

First Edition

Britannica Educational Publishing
J.E. Luebering: Director, Core Reference Group
Anthony L. Green: Editor, Compton's by Britannica

Rosen Publishing
Hope Lourie Killcoyne: Executive Editor
Kathy Kuhtz Campbell: Senior Editor
Nelson Sá: Art Director
Nicole Russo: Designer
Cindy Reiman: Photography Manager
Introduction and supplementary material by Kara Rogers

**Library of Congress Cataloging-in-Publication Data**

Cloning/edited by Kara Rogers.—First edition.
pages cm.—(The biotechnology revolution)
Includes bibliographical references and index.
ISBN 978-1-62275-576-9 (library bound)
1. Cloning—Juvenile literature. 2. Genetic engineering—Juvenile literature. 3. Medical genetics—Juvenile literature. I. Rogers, Kara, editor.
QH442.2.C563 2016
660.6'5—dc23

2014048919

*Manufactured in the United States of America*

**Photo credits:** Cover, p.1 nevodka/Shutterstock.com; p. vii Imagno/Hulton Archive/Getty Images; p. 4 Big Cheese Photo/Thinkstock; pp. 6-7, 20-21, 43, 51, 53, 72, 74, 80-81 Encyclopædia Britannica, Inc.; p. 9 Nigel Cattlin/ Science Source; p. 15 Daniel Naupold/picture-alliance/dpa/AP Images; pp. 24-25 Press Association/AP Images; p. 48 Martin Shields/Science Source; p. 56 Carlos Goldin/Science Source; p. 65 Emi/Shutterstock.com; pp. 84, 114-115, 143 © AP Images; pp. 88, 122-123 James King-Holmes/Science Source; pp. 92-93 David Greedy/Getty Images; p. 101 AdstockRF; p. 103 Getty Images; p. 108 Reuters/Landov; pp. 124-125 Glen Stubbe/MCT/Landov; p. 127 Jerry Lampen/Reuters/Landov; pp. 132-133 Mario Tama/Getty Images; pp. 146-147 Chip Somodevilla/Getty Images News/ Thinkstock; p. 150 Kyodo/AP Images; pp. 154-155 © Nelvin C. Cepeda/SDU-T/ZUMA Press; cover and interior design elements vitstudio/Shutterstock.com (DNA), everythingpossible/iStock/Thinkstock (honeycomb), style_TTT/Shutterstock.com (linear patterns).

# CONTENTS

# INTRODUCTION

The process of generating a living entity that is a genetic duplicate of another is known as cloning. The science and technology behind that process are powerful. They have the potential to treat human disease, to improve agriculture, and to advance scientists' understanding of basic cellular processes.

The benefits of those advances to humankind could be immense. But the use of cloning technologies also raises significant ethical issues. Of particular concern has been the use of human embryos for the generation of cloned stem cells—the cells that form the basis of therapeutic cloning—and the potential of reproductive cloning to produce genetically identical copies of humans.

Therapeutic cloning and reproductive cloning are derived from more than a century of research and development. Reproductive cloning, in which the objective is to create an individual organism that is a genetic copy of another individual, generally is considered to have begun with the work of German embryologist Hans Spemann, who in the early 1900s artificially "twinned" salamanders. Spemann created twin salamanders by constricting salamander zygotes (fertilized eggs), such that in each egg, the cell nucleus was forced to one side, leaving the other half of the egg enucleated (without a nucleus). He let the zygote grow through several rounds of cell division before releasing the constriction to allow a single cell nucleus to slip into the enucleated side. He then closed off the constriction, cutting the embryo in two. The result was the generation of twin offspring. Spemann's work laid the foundation for nuclear transfer, the process by which the nucleus of a cell is inserted into an enucleated egg cell. Nuclear transfer is at the centre of cloning technology.

*German embryologist Hans Spemann was the first to carry out reproductive cloning by artificial "twinning," or embryo splitting, which he performed on a salamander embryo in the early 1900s.*

The northern leopard frog (*Lithobates pipiens*, formerly *Rana pipiens*) was one of the first species to be cloned through nuclear transfer. Cloned tadpoles were generated from embryonic cells in the early 1950s. Later that decade, the first tadpole clones of the African clawed frog (*Xenopus laevis*) were produced. Rather than embryonic cells, however, the cloned tadpoles of the clawed frog were produced from the nuclei of adult (differentiated) cells of the frog intestine. The experiment indicated that egg cells had the ability to make the nuclei of old cells young again—a process in which adult cell nuclei essentially are reprogrammed to a pluripotent state. With a pluripotent nucleus at the helm, a cell has the capacity to become any type of cell in the body. It took about two decades to verify the experiments that produced tadpole clones of the African clawed frog. But once proven, the gateway to the cloning of larger species was opened.

In parallel with that work, there occurred other key developments in the biological sciences that fueled the advance of cloning technology. Central among them was the development in the 1970s of recombinant DNA technology, in which a piece of DNA of interest is cut out of the genome of one organism and inserted into the genome of another organism. Numerous copies of the DNA of interest can be created by inserting the recombined genome into replicating bacterial cells. Advances in recombinant DNA technology and DNA sequencing gave rise to gene cloning, which became the most widely used type of cloning technology. Gene cloning is important particularly in the production of genetically modified organisms, which have a wide array of applications in research, medicine, and agriculture.

In the 1980s, while some scientists worked to refine the process of gene cloning, others found ways to successfully apply embryo cloning techniques to mammals. The first cloned mammals were sheep, produced in 1984 through nuclear transfer with embryonic cells derived from eight-cell embryos. Scientists attempted mammalian cloning with embryonic cells in later stages of development, but all the clones produced in that way were still clones of embryonic origin—they were not clones of adult animals. Indeed, that singular breakthrough—the generation of an animal that is a genetic replica of an already grown individual—remained elusive.

Eventually, scientists came to realize that the key to cloning mammals from adult cells was timing. The DNA in the nuclei of adult cells had to be in a receptive state, open to signals for development that came from the egg environment. A way of forcing adult cell nuclei into that state was devised in 1996, when scientists produced the world's first mammalian clone of an adult animal. The clone was a Finn Dorset sheep named Dolly. Her birth marked the culmination of decades of progress in cloning technology, as well as years of research into mammalian embryological development and reproduction.

The technique used to produce Dolly became known as somatic cell nuclear transfer (SCNT). Though it had undergone significant refinement, the idea of

SCNT was derived from the work that produced the first cloned tadpoles of the African clawed frog. SCNT formed the basis for all subsequent major milestones in the advance of cloning science, including, crucially, the development of methods to produce patient-specific stem cells.

Stem cells by definition are undifferentiated. They divide to produce daughter cells, some of which remain in an immature, undifferentiated state and others of which become specialized through the process of differentiation, ultimately maturing into the more than 200 different cell types that make up the human body. Among the most versatile stem cells are embryonic stem cells (ESCs), which are deeply undifferentiated, existing in a state of pluripotency. Pluripotency is vital to the development of effective stem-cell therapies—stem cells intended to replace diseased or defective cells must be able to develop into the needed cell type. Central to the development of patient-specific stem-cell therapy, in which the stem cells used for transplantation possess the same DNA as the other cells in the patient's body, is therapeutic cloning.

Therapeutic cloning centres on the use of SCNT, which scientists have shown is capable of producing human ESCs that are clones of adult cells from patients. Following the transfer of the nucleus of the adult cell into an enucleated egg cell, the reconstructed embryo is allowed to develop only to the blastocyst stage, at which point the ESCs are isolated.

The ESCs could then be used for transplants, being injected into the patient's body to treat a wide array of diseases and disorders. Because the stem cells would be genetically the same as the patient's existing body cells, they could reduce the risk of immune rejection, a complication that can undermine the success of cell transplantation with donor cells.

Human ESCs were isolated for the first time in 1998, a development that opened up tremendous opportunities for research and medicine. But because human embryos are destroyed in the process of isolating ESCs, their use in research is highly contentious. Some people fear that the application of SCNT to generate human ESCs could be abused—that the embryo derived from the technique would not be destroyed, that it would be implanted into a woman's uterus and carried to term, producing a human clone of an adult. As a result, many governments have banned the use of human embryos for the generation of ESCs. Consequently, research into ESCs for cell transplantation and the use of SCNT to clone ESCs from the adult cells of patients with disease has progressed very slowly. Few clinical trials have been approved to test the safety and effectiveness of stem cell transplantation. The process of producing ESCs from human embryos with SCNT also has proven exceptionally difficult, with few successful attempts reported.

In the early 2000s, scientists found a new way of producing stem cells for research—an approach that circumvented the use of human embryos. Instead of using embryos, scientists inserted genes into the nuclei of adult cells. The genes caused the cells to revert from a differentiated state to a pluripotent state. Such cells became known as induced-pluripotent stem (iPS) cells. Although their promise is great, whether iPS cells possess the same abilities and potential as ESCs is unclear. In general, ESCs appear to have greater potential for differentiation than iPS cells, and their generation does not involve direct manipulation of the genome, suggesting that ESCs may be safer than iPS cells. Very little is known about the differentiation potential and safety of stem cells produced with SCNT.

In the following chapters, readers will explore the history, the science, the applications, and the ethical issues of cloning. Along that journey, readers will discover the promise and potential of cloning technology. They will learn of the occurrence of cloning in nature and of the many ways in which animals and plants reproduce—processes that are fundamental to an understanding of the basis of artificial cloning. Chapters devoted to reproductive and therapeutic cloning offer detailed discussion of the technology, biology, and uses of artificial cloning. The final chapter explores the ethical, social, and moral controversies of cloning. No other area of biotechnology is so ethically conflicted as the science of cloning—a reflection of the power inherent in the technologies behind it.

CHAPTER ONE

# CLONING DEFINED AND MAJOR DEVELOPMENTS IN THE HISTORY OF CLONING

A clone (also spelled clon) is a cell or organism that is genetically identical to the original cell or organism from which it is derived. The word *clone* originates from the ancient Greek *klon*, meaning "twig."

*Clone* is a relatively modern term. It was introduced in 1903 by American plant scientist Herbert J. Webber, who used it in reference to plants that had been produced through asexual (vegetative) propagation by horticultural methods—twig cuttings are a source of material for the cultivation of certain plant species. Plants that are propagated asexually, whether from twigs or cuttings of other parts or from bulbs or buds, are exact genetic replicas of their parent plant. They are, in other words, clones.

Clones have been commonplace in horticulture since ancient times. Many varieties of plants, in fact, are cloned simply by obtaining cuttings of their leaves, stems, or roots and replanting them. A vast array of fruit and nut tree varieties and innumerable ornamental plants represent clones. In essence, those clones are the products of artificial cloning—the application of techniques and methods to generate a genetically identical copy of a cell or an organism. Artificial cloning is contrasted to cloning that occurs naturally.

## CLONING IN NATURE

Cloning happens all the time in nature. Plants that are able to reproduce by asexual means naturally, for example, give rise to new individuals that are genetically identical to the parent plant. A cell that replicates itself asexually without any genetic alteration or recombination also is a clone.

Prokaryotic organisms (organisms that lack a cell nucleus), such as bacteria, for example, create genetic duplicates of themselves using forms of asexual reproduction known as binary fission and budding. In eukaryotic organisms (organisms possessing a cell nucleus) such as humans, all the cells that undergo mitosis, such as skin cells and cells lining the gastrointestinal tract, are clones. The only exceptions are gametes (eggs and sperm), which undergo meiosis and genetic recombination.

## NATURAL CLONING PROCESSES IN HUMANS

The replication of cells in humans is a striking example of the extent to which cloning occurs in nature. The identical genetic makewup of cells that divide through mitosis in the human body is derived from their shared embryonic origin. In humans, the fertilized egg from which an individual develops contains DNA from both the mother and the father. The egg divides into two identical cells, then four, then eight, and so on. Those cells are clones. The DNA within them is cloned—it is copied into every cell that is produced. In time, the cells begin to differentiate, or become specialized. They develop, for example, into skin cells, eye cells, liver cells, and muscle cells. Amazingly, despite differentiation, the cells remain genetically identical—each cell has the same DNA as the original fertilized egg.

The differentiation of cells into different types is the result of changes not in the DNA itself (mutations, for example) but rather in how the cells use, or express, their genes. Many of the genes in a cell become inactive through the differentiation process. Only the genes that are needed by each type of specialized cell to stay alive and perform its specific functions are expressed. As the specialized cells multiply and organize to form their distinct tissues, organs, and other structures, even more clones of cells are formed. In that rough sense, most living things are mainly groups of cloned cells. For their entire lives, organisms clone cells and their DNA. The process is vital to the growth of organisms, to their ability to heal after cell-destroying injury, and to their ability to replace cells that die naturally.

Another example of cloning at work in humans is the phenomenon of identical twins (or triplets). Such individuals are clones, in that they are produced from

*Identical twins are an example of natural cloning. Such twins come from the same fertilized egg. The hereditary material from which they originate is absolutely identical in every way. Although they look almost identical in appearance, their fingerprints are different.*

the same fertilized egg and are therefore made up of genetically identical cells. Identical twins are clones of one another, rather than clones of the parent.

## NATURAL CLONING PROCESSES IN PLANTS

Cloning in complex, multicellular plants can occur through any of several natural processes, all of which are methods of asexual reproduction. One such method involves the growth of runners, specialized stemlike structures that sprout young plants that are genetically identical to the plant from which they grow. The young plants develop roots, sink them into the soil, and become self-sustaining. The ancestor plant and all the plants that spring from it via runners make up a clone. Strawberry is an example of a plant that is capable of producing runners.

The production of tubers is another way in which certain species of plants can clone themselves. Tubers are short, thickened stems that reside mostly beneath the ground and that constitute the resting stage of certain seed plants. Tubers bear minute scale leaves, each with a bud that has the potential for developing into a new plant. Potato plants, for example, can reproduce asexually through the growth of tubers, or potatoes (the edible portion of the plant). The "eyes" of the potato are the nodes from which new plants grow. When a whole potato or part of a potato with nodes is planted, it will give rise to one or more new plants—all of which are clones of the individual that produced the potato used for planting.

## REGENERATION

A less common form of natural cloning is regeneration. In regeneration, pieces cut from an organism

*Some animals, such as sea stars, can regrow missing parts through regeneration. As long as a portion of a sea star's body, or disk, remains associated with an arm, a sea star can regenerate.*

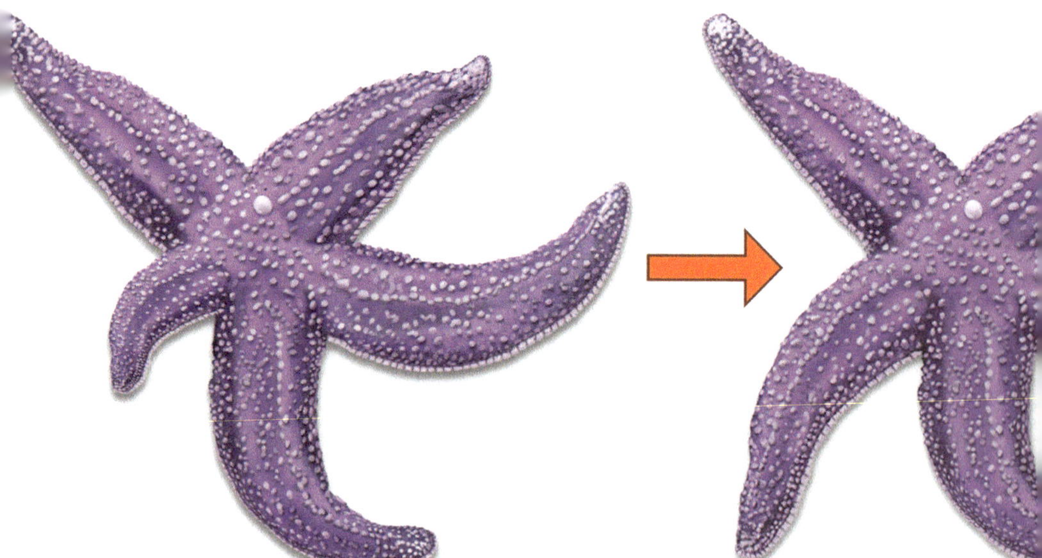

**Regeneration**

grow into whole new organisms. Such is the case with some sea stars (commonly known as starfish), whose bodies can be cut into several pieces with the result that each piece grows into a complete sea star. Each of the resulting sea stars is genetically identical to the others, so they all are clones of the original sea star.

## ARTIFICIAL CLONING

Because there are enormous actual and potential advantages in areas such as agriculture, medicine, and biological research in producing genetically identical organisms, artificial cloning has been a focus of attention in science. Many varieties of fruits and nuts, for example, owe their predictable uniformity of taste, appearance, shipping characteristics, and more to cloning.

A useful example of the application of cloning in agriculture is the production of certain varieties of apples. All McIntosh apples, for instance, are produced from trees that have been grafted with tree parts that can be traced to ideal McIntosh trees developed generations ago. Grafting is a relatively simple process. The stems of two plants are cut off, then the stem of the plant with the desired fruit is grafted onto the place where the other stem was cut. Done properly, the process results in the successful healing of the two parts together and the grafted stem producing branches that are genetically identical to the ancestor tree. Those branches, therefore, grow apples much like those from the ideal ancestor trees.

In biomedical research, cloning is broadly defined to mean the duplication of any kind of biological material for scientific study, such as a piece of DNA or an individual cell. Segments of DNA can be replicated exponentially, for example, by a process known as polymerase chain reaction (PCR), a technique that is used widely in basic biological research.

The ability to clone genes that direct the production of medically significant substances contributes to the advance of treatments for disease. After such a gene is isolated, it can be inserted into a special construct known as a plasmid and replicated in a bacterium or it can be inserted into a tissue cell to be duplicated during the development of an animal embryo into the cells of the resulting adult. When achieved and when the gene is shown to function normally (or can be made to do so), the bacterial or tissue culture or the animal (and some or all of its offspring) become a kind of "factory" for making the desired substance. The process has been achieved for the production of medically significant substances such as insulin, growth hormone, interferon, and antithrombin.

Scientists also have been able to produce genetically identical organisms for scientific study and experimentation. Through repeated inbreeding,

*In this example of artificial cloning in agriculture, a pink flowering apple tree part has been grafted to a white flowering variety. Grafting is used for various purposes, such as repairing injured trees, strengthening plants' resistance to certain diseases, and ensuring pollination.*

or the breeding of closely related individuals, scientists can produce animals that are near-clones. Such work has produced, for example, many strains of mice that essentially are genetically identical—males are identical and females are identical. Mice that are near-clones of one another are in demand by scientists worldwide, since the use of such animals helps minimize confusing differences in results that are caused by differences in genetic makeup from one individual to another.

Inbreeding, however, does not produce perfect clones. Rather, the production of actual clones of complex animals has proven extraordinarily difficult. That type of cloning, in which the goal is to produce clones of whole animals, is known as reproductive cloning. Reproductive cloning has long challenged scientists, and it has raised troubling questions about its ethical, religious, and moral significance. On the one hand is the promise of herds of ideal farm animals that efficiently produce milk, meat, and eggs of just the type desired. On the other hand, there is the specter of cloning humans, a possibility so fraught with difficult questions that many countries banned work on such cloning.

## EARLY CLONING EXPERIMENTS

Reproductive cloning originally was carried out by artificial "twinning," or embryo splitting. One of the first successes of embryo splitting was recorded in the early 1900s, when German embryologist Hans Spemann split a salamander embryo to produce two identical animals. In the ensuing decades, Spemann, who was later awarded the Nobel Prize for Physiology or Medicine (1935) for his research on embryonic development, theorized about another cloning procedure, one known as nuclear transfer, in which the nucleus, which contains the genes, is removed from an egg cell and replaced with the nucleus from another cell. At the time, such a possibility was pure fancy, for the tools and techniques that could accomplish such a procedure did not exist.

In 1952 American scientists Robert W. Briggs and Thomas J. King managed to take the nucleus out of the cell of a frog embryo and insert it into an enucleated frog egg. They worked with the frog *Rana pipiens*, the eggs of which were considered ideal for such work at the time because they are relatively large and therefore easier to manipulate than those of many other animals, including mammals. The researchers used nuclei from partially differentiated cells for their experiments. Their efforts, however, consistently resulted in the production of abnormal frog embryos.

Just six years later, British biologist John Bertrand Gurdon successfully carried out nuclear transfer using DNA from adult intestinal cells of African clawed frogs (*Xenopus laevis*). Given the outcome of Briggs and King's work, however, Gurdon's results met with

# SIR JOHN BERTRAND GURDON

Sir John Bertrand Gurdon was born on October 2, 1933, at Dippenhall, in Hampshire, England. A developmental biologist, Sir John Bertrand Gurdon was the first to demonstrate that egg cells are able to reprogram differentiated cell nuclei, reverting them to a pluripotent state, in which they regain the capacity to become any type of cell. Gurdon's work ultimately came to form the foundation for major advances in cloning and stem cell research, including the generation of Dolly—the first mammal successfully cloned from a differentiated cell—by British developmental biologist Sir Ian Wilmut and the discovery of induced pluripotent stem (iPS) cells by Japanese physician and researcher Shinya Yamanaka—an advance that revolutionized the field of regenerative medicine. For his discoveries, Gurdon was awarded the 2012 Nobel Prize in Physiology or Medicine, which he shared with Yamanaka.

Gurdon studied classics (ancient Greek and Roman language and literature) as a student at Eton College, a prestigious secondary school for boys near Windsor, England. He intended to continue his classics studies at Christ Church, Oxford, but was not accepted to the program. Instead, after being tutored in zoology, he gained acceptance to that department at Oxford, earning a B.S. in 1956. That year he began his graduate studies in the laboratory of embryologist Michail Fischberg and initiated a series of experiments on nuclear transfer in the African clawed frog (*Xenopus laevis*). He proceeded to generate cloned tadpoles from differentiated *Xenopus* intestinal cell nuclei, demonstrating that egg cells could undifferentiate previously differentiated nuclei and that normal embryos could be produced with the technique. He published his seminal findings in 1958. However, because American scientists Robert Briggs and Thomas King previously had found that the transfer of nuclei from partially differentiated cells consistently resulted in the production of abnormal embryos in the frog *Rana pipiens*, Gurdon's results were greeted with skepticism.

After completing a Ph.D. in 1960, Gurdon received a yearlong postdoctoral fellowship to conduct research at the California Institute of Technology in Pasadena, where he investigated the genetics of bacteria-infecting viruses (bacteriophages). He then returned to Oxford, becoming a faculty member in the zoology department and continuing his work to characterize nuclear changes that take place during cell differentiation.

In 1971 Gurdon joined the Medical Research Council Laboratory of Molecular Biology (LMB) in Cambridge, and in 1979 he became the head of the LMBs division of cell biology. While there he worked to identify the molecules in egg cells that were responsible for the nuclear reprogramming effect. Also during that time, other scientists began to confirm the results of Gurdon's early experiments with *Xenopus*, which effectively solidified his position as a leader in nuclear transfer. In 1983 he took a professorship in cell biology at the University of Cambridge. He later moved to the Wellcome Trust/Cancer Research Campaign Institute

*(continued on the next page)*

(continued from the previous page)

(later the Wellcome Trust/Cancer Research UK Gurdon Institute), a Cambridge-based institution that he cofounded in 1989 and that in 2004 was named for him. He directed the institute until 2001, after which he focused on research full-time.

Gurdon received numerous awards throughout his career—notably, in addition to the 2012 Nobel Prize, the 1985 Royal Medal of the Royal Society, the 2003 Copley Medal of the Royal Society, and the 2009 Albert Lasker Basic Medical Research Award (shared with Yamanaka). He was made a fellow of the Royal Society in 1971 and a foreign associate of the U.S. National Academy of Sciences in 1980. He was knighted in 1995.

skepticism. Through the 1970s, other scientists tried procedures that were the same or similar to the one employed by Gurdon. Eventually, that work validated Gurdon's results, but years of failed experiments in mammals ensued. Some scientists began to wonder whether animals more complex than frogs could be cloned.

## THE DEVELOPMENT OF RECOMBINANT DNA TECHNOLOGY

At the same time, other developments in biotechnology were occurring that ultimately would come to bear on cloning. Advancements in the field of molecular biology were especially critical, leading, for example, to the development of techniques that allowed scientists to manipulate cells and to detect chemical markers that signal changes within cells. With the advent of recombinant DNA technology in the 1970s, it became possible for scientists to cut out select fragments of DNA, recombine them with DNA from other organisms, and insert the recombined molecules into rapidly multiplying bacterial cells to produce millions of

*A scientist holds an African clawed frog during embryonic cell research. In 1958, John B. Gurdon successfully carried out nuclear transfer using DNA from adult intestinal cells of African clawed frogs.*

copies of the select DNA fragment. That process became known as gene, or DNA, cloning.

A key step that preceded the development of recombinant DNA technology was the discovery of restriction enzymes in 1968 by Swiss microbiologist Werner Arber. However, type II restriction enzymes, which are essential to gene cloning for their ability to cleave a specific site within the DNA (as opposed to type I restriction enzymes, which cleave DNA at random sites), were not identified until 1969, when American molecular biologist Hamilton O. Smith purified the enzyme. Drawing on Smith's work, American molecular biologist Daniel Nathans made critical progress in the technique of DNA recombination in 1970–71 and demonstrated that type II enzymes could be useful in genetic studies. Arber, Smith, and Nathans shared the 1978 Nobel Prize for Physiology or Medicine for their discoveries concerning restriction enzymes.

Other researchers were quick to make use of the then newly described restriction enzymes, and in 1973 American biochemists Stanley N. Cohen and Herbert W. Boyer pioneered recombinant DNA technology. They were among the first scientists to cut DNA into fragments, rejoin different fragments, and insert the new genes into *E. coli* bacteria, which then reproduced.

The development of DNA cloning was followed by advances in DNA sequencing, which allowed scientists to deduce the nucleotide patterns—the A (adenine), T (thymine), C (cytosine), and G (guanine) codes—of genes. The techniques originally used for gene cloning were difficult to perform. They were also time-consuming. But in the 1980s, with the invention of PCR by American biochemist Kary B. Mullis, scientists were able to clone genes and analyze DNA with unprecedented speed. PCR allows a specific stretch of DNA to be copied billions of times in just a matter of hours. Its development was so significant, that Mullis received a share of the 1993 Nobel Prize for Chemistry for his work.

Advances in recombinant DNA technology were accompanied by progress in scientists' understanding of cloning techniques as they applied to animals. Scientists had begun to realize, for example, the importance to success of the exact age of the genetic material used for nuclear transfer. Experiments with cells in relatively late stages of embryonic development—at three cell divisions from the fertilized egg, for example—failed to produce clones in various animal species. The evidence suggested that the more differentiated that a cell becomes, the less able it is to respond to signals within the egg environment.

Indeed, once a fertilized egg begins to divide and thereby begins the process that results in the formation of an embryo, the resulting cells are on a kind of schedule that gradually brings them to their specialized states. As the cells differentiate, however, genes that are not necessary to the specialized functions of the cells are turned off. And as a consequence of that process, when the nucleus of a differentiated cell is inserted into an enucleated egg, the genes are not in the proper stage or condition to respond the egg's instructions. To develop into an embryo and, eventually, a complete organism, the egg requires an open, unsuppressed set of genes.

## THE FIRST CLONED MAMMALS

In 1984 Danish-born embryologist Steen Willadsen successfully cloned sheep using nuclear transfer with cells from eight-cell embryos, marking a major advance in cloning science. The cloned sheep were produced by combining cells from eight-cell embryos with enucleated eggs from donor ewes. The resulting blastocysts were transferred to recipient ewes, which subsequently gave birth to full-term lambs. The lambs were clones of the sheep from which the eight-cell embryos were derived. Willadsen's experiments were validated by other scientists, and clones of other mammals, including cows and pigs, were produced in the years afterward. All were the products of cloning from early and partially differentiated embryonic cells.

A major reason for cloning livestock is to produce animals with superior qualities, such as increased growth rate, reduced body fat, or high milk production. Hence, individual animals that naturally possess such qualities are targets of reproductive cloning. Before scientists could generate such clones, however, they needed to find a way to clone animals from differentiated cells, such as skin or muscle cells. For, those cells, unlike embryonic cells produced by combining the genomes of two individuals, contained only the genome of the individual to be cloned.

Indications that mammals could be cloned from differentiated cells emerged in the 1990s, when researchers successfully produced mammalian clones from cultured cell lines. The first to do so were American scientists Michelle Sims and Neal L. First, who in 1994 reported the production of cloned calves from embryonic cells that had been maintained in cell culture for less than a month. The cells were at least several divisions from the initial fertilized egg. The result raised the possibility that differentiated cells might one day be used for cloning.

A hypothesis proposed for the success of the experiments centred on quiescence, or a state of cellular inactivity. By culturing the cells, using specialized culture media, and thereby interrupting the cells' schedule of growth and differentiation, the cells became stressed. As a result, they entered into an inactive state. Scientists suspected that during that time, the cells' chromatin structure was modified, such that the DNA was rendered responsive to instructions present in the egg environment. Through quiescence, then, cells became susceptible to dedifferentiation. Adult cells, in other words, could be made young again,

Dolly: The Cloning of a Sheep, 1996

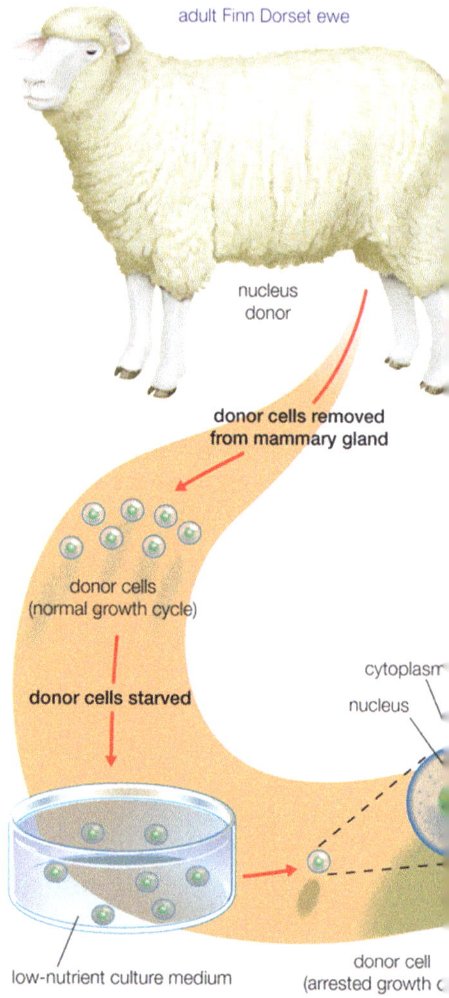


regaining pluripotency—the potential of an embryonic cell to grow into any one of the numerous different types of somatic cells that make up a complete organism. In a pluripotent state, scientists surmised, the cells would be subject to nuclear reprogramming by the egg environment, a process that in turn enabled development.

In 1996 British developmental biologist Ian Wilmut and colleagues at the Roslin Institute near Edinburgh, Scotland, reasoned that nutrient deprivation could cause relatively advanced embryonic cells to become quiescent and thereby dedifferentiate. To test their idea, the researchers established embryonic cells in cell culture conditions, allowing

*Dolly the sheep was cloned using a process called somatic cell nuclear transfer (SCNT). The technique resulted in the creation of a genetically identical clone of an already grown sheep.*

the cells to undergo several rounds of division. They then drastically reduced nutrients available to the cells for several days before removing the cell nuclei and inserting the nuclei into enucleated eggs. The success of the method was proven by the birth of lamb clones.

That same year, Wilmut and his team of scientists produced Dolly, a cloned sheep generated through nuclear transfer involving an enucleated embryo and a differentiated, adult cell. The adult cells were isolated from the mammary gland of a six-year-old Finn Dorset ewe and grown in cell culture, where the researchers provided the cells with very little nourishment. Then, using an electrical pulse, they caused each cell to fuse with an enucleated egg cell from another ewe. The nucleus of the mammary cell was transferred into the egg. The electrical pulse also caused the egg cell to begin to divide.

When the reconstructed embryos reached their sixth day, they were implanted into the uteri of healthy female sheep. Of the 277 embryos produced through cell fusion and nuclear transfer, only one completed the developmental journey—an embryo that gave rise to Dolly, a clone of the Finn Dorset ewe from which the mammary cells originally were collected. For the first time, a complex animal had been cloned from a fully differentiated cell. Dolly's development and birth were normal (though she was euthanized in February 2003, after having been found to suffer from progressive lung disease).

## CLONING EXPERIMENTS WITH HUMAN EMBRYOS

The announcement of Dolly's birth in late February 1997 stunned many scientists and revived controversy over the cloning of humans. At the time, simply proving that a mammalian clone could be produced was a significant step. Once that feat was achieved, most scientists reasoned that refinement of the techniques used would almost surely increase the rate of success in mammalian cloning.

Just days after the announcement of the success with Dolly, a research team in Oregon produced two identical rhesus monkey clones from the cells of a single embryo. Although the twinned monkeys were produced from embryonic cells (rather than adult cells), they were the closest evolutionary relatives to humans ever to be cloned. The results, taken together with Dolly, seemed to point toward what might be the inevitable cloning of humans.

## SIR IAN WILMUT

Sir Ian Wilmut was born on July 7, 1944, at Hampton Lucy, in Warwickshire, England. Wilmut, a developmental biologist, was the first to use nuclear transfer of differentiated adult cells to generate a mammalian clone, the Finn Dorset sheep named Dolly, born in 1996.

## EDUCATION AND CRYOPRESERVATION RESEARCH

Wilmut was raised in Coventry, a town in the historic English county of Warwickshire, and he attended the Agricultural College at the University of Nottingham. In his undergraduate studies, Wilmut initially pursued his lifelong interest in farming, particularly in raising animals such as sheep. However, he soon turned his attention to animal science and basic research. In 1966, his final year at Nottingham, he received a scholarship to conduct research for a summer under English biologist Ernest John Christopher Polge in the Unit of Reproductive Physiology and Biochemistry, then a division of the Agricultural Research Council at the University of Cambridge. During that time, Wilmut performed basic experiments on animal embryos.

Following his graduation from Nottingham in 1967, he

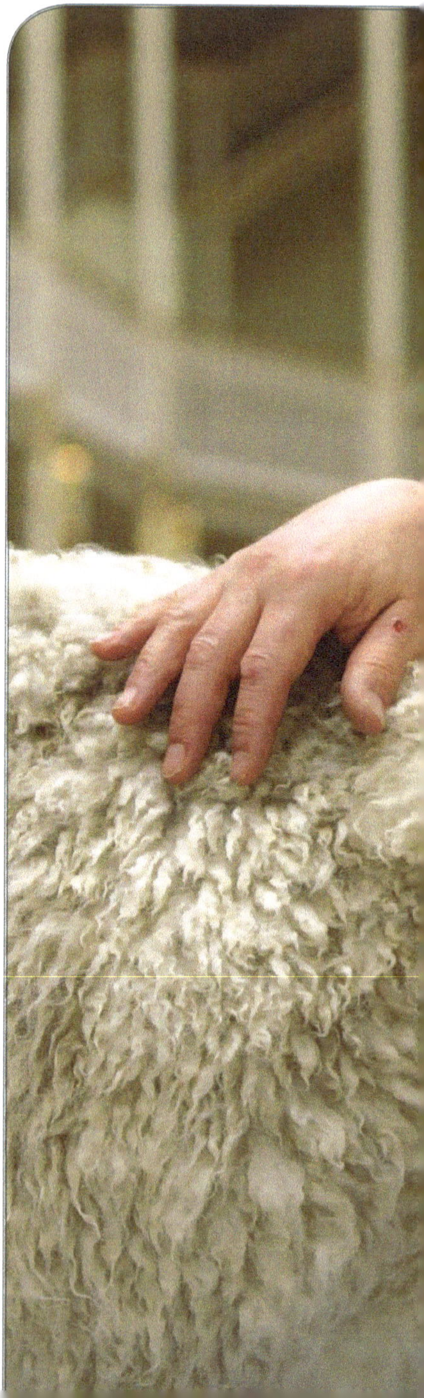

*Sir Ian Wilmut poses here with Dolly, the world's first cloned sheep, who, after her death in 2003, was put on display at the National Museum of Scotland in Edinburgh.*

returned to Cambridge, where he pursued a doctorate under the guidance of Polge, whose research was focused on improving methods of embryo cryopreservation. In 1971 Wilmut was awarded a doctorate by Darwin College, Cambridge. He remained at Cambridge and conducted extensive research on the cryopreservation of embryos. In 1973 he successfully implanted into a surrogate cow a calf embryo that had been cryopreserved. The embryo was carried to term, and Wilmut named the first-ever "frozen calf" Frostie.

## GENETIC ENGINEERING AND CLONING RESEARCH

In 1973 Wilmut was appointed senior scientific officer at the Animal Breeding Research Organisation (ABRO; renamed Edinburgh Research Station of the Institute of Animal Physiology and Genetics Research in 1985 and finally Roslin Institute in 1993), a government-supported research facility located in Roslin, Scotland, just south of Edinburgh. At the ABRO facility, Wilmut studied embryo development and became interested in the underlying causes of embryo death in mammals. However, in the early 1980s, changes in ABRO leadership and a shift in the focus of government research projects forced Wilmut into the realm of genetic engineering. The new goal of ABRO was to generate sheep genetically engineered to produce large quantities of human proteins that would be suitable for therapeutic uses, a pursuit that came to be known as "pharming."

Although Wilmut had little experience with genetic engineering and had limited enthusiasm for the project, he used his knowledge of developmental biology to obtain zygotes (one-celled embryos) from sheep and developed techniques to inject DNA into the zygote pronucleus (a haploid nucleus occurring in embryos prior to fertilization). The work eventually led to the generation of a sheep named Tracy. Tracy was created from a zygote genetically engineered through DNA injection to produce milk containing large quantities of the human enzyme alpha-1 antitrypsin, a substance used to treat cystic fibrosis and emphysema.

Wilmut's initial forays into cloning began in the late 1980s with embryonic stem cells. He and his colleagues were interested primarily in nuclear transfer, and in 1989 with Lawrence Smith, a graduate student conducting his thesis research at Roslin, Wilmut generated four cloned lambs with embryonic cell nuclear transfer, in which the nucleus from an embryonic stem cell was inserted into an enucleated egg. The research led Wilmut and Smith to an important discovery—namely, that the stage of the cell cycle (the sequence through which each cell progresses from one cell division to the next) at the time of nuclear transfer determined the success or failure of the experiment. They realized that the four clones they had generated happened by chance.

In 1991 Wilmut hired English biologist Keith Campbell, whose knowledge of the cell cycle proved instrumental in advancing the technique of nuclear transfer developed at Roslin. Wilmut and Campbell's first major success came in 1995, with the generation of two cloned Welsh mountain sheep, Megan and Morag. The following year Wilmut, Campbell, and their team of scientists decided to test a new theory based on the idea that the age or the stage of differentiation of a donor cell did not matter in nuclear transfer. Prior to that theory, nuclear transfer was believed to work only if the nucleus used as the donor for nuclear transfer came from a cell that was totipotent—a cell that had the ability to differentiate into any type of cell in the body and that could give rise to extraembryonic (placental) cells. Totipotent cells, therefore, possessed no characteristics of differentiation. However, observations from laboratory experiments and from Megan and Morag, who were produced using nine-day-old embryonic cells (which presumably are pluripotent, or less totipotent than younger embryonic cells) indicated that an enucleated host egg could somehow reverse the differentiation of the donor cell nucleus, converting it back to a state of totipotency or pluripotency. That indication led to the idea of using the nucleus from an already differentiated adult cell as a donor nucleus.

During the winter of 1995–96, Wilmut was involved in three pivotal cloning experiments conducted at Roslin. In the first, he and his team of scientists performed embryonic cell nuclear transfer by using cultured embryonic cells that were nine days old. The experiment was similar to the experiment that led to the creation of Megan and Morag. However, the new experiment involved a different sheep breed—the cells used for nuclear transfer came from a Poll Dorset sheep. The test resulted in the birth in 1996 of four Poll Dorset clones: Cedric, Cecil, Cyril, and Tuppence.

In the second experiment, the team used fetal fibroblasts isolated from sheep fetuses after twenty-six days of development. The cells served as nucleus donors for transfer into an enucleated egg. The experiment resulted in the birth of two clones, Taffy and Tweed.

In the third experiment, the scientists isolated adult cells (in this case, mammary gland cells) from a six-year-old Finn Dorset ewe and used the cells as nucleus donors for transfer into egg cells. Wilmut and his team constructed 277 embryos containing adult cell nuclei that were implanted into thirteen surrogate mothers, only one of which became pregnant. The pregnancy was carried to term successfully. The Finn Dorset lamb, born on July 5, 1996, was Dolly.

In 1997, following the publication of a summary of their research leading to Dolly, Wilmut, Campbell, and the Roslin Institute instantly became known for having opened the door to a new era of cloning research. The cloning of Dolly generated speculation in the media and in the scientific community about the possibility of cloning humans. Wilmut considered human cloning impractical for both ethical and scientific reasons. From his work with sheep, he knew the dangers of cloning. Many embryos died following implantation, and those embryos that survived and developed to term as full-grown fetuses sometimes died immediately following birth or were born with birth defects.

Wilmut was not interested in cloning simply for the sake of producing cloned animals, and neither was his team of scientists at Roslin. They still had problems to solve concerning their work on pharming. In 1997 Wilmut and his colleagues generated Polly, a Poll Dorset clone made from nuclear transfer using a fetal fibroblast nucleus genetically engineered to express a human gene known as FIX. The gene encodes a substance called human factor IX, a clotting factor that occurs naturally in most people but is absent in people with hemophilia, who require replacement therapy with a therapeutic form of the substance. Polly—along with two other sheep engineered to produce human factor IX that also were born in 1997—represented a major advance in pharming. The successful birth of Polly marked Wilmut's last major cloning experiment.

## LATER CAREER

Throughout Wilmut's career at Roslin, he had been slowly moving away from research relying on embryonic stem cells, primarily because culturing embryonic stem cells from sheep embryos was extraordinarily difficult and impractical in terms of cost and time. In 2000 Wilmut was promoted to head of the department of gene expression and development at the Roslin Institute, and his research interests shifted from animals to humans. He was particularly interested in uncovering the genetic mechanisms that control embryonic development and the role that these mechanisms play in human disease. In 2005 he accepted a position as chair of reproductive science at the University of Edinburgh. He maintained a relationship with the Roslin Institute, acting as a visiting scientist. Wilmut also directed the Medical Research Council's Centre for Regenerative Medicine, located in Edinburgh, and led research efforts into cellular reprogramming.

Wilmut received several awards during his career, including the Ernst Schering prize in 2002 and the Paul Ehrlich and Ludwig Darmstaedter prize in 2005. Wilmut also was made fellow of the Royal Society of Edinburgh in 2000 and of the Royal Society of London in 2002. He was knighted in 2007. In addition to papers published in high-ranking journals such as *Nature* and

*Science*, Wilmut also published several books, including *The Second Creation: Dolly and the Age of Biological Control* (2000; with Keith Campbell and Colin Tudge) and *After Dolly: The Uses and Misuses of Human Cloning* (2006; with Roger Highfield).

## DEVELOPMENTS AFTER DOLLY

The technique used to produce Dolly became known as somatic cell nuclear transfer (SCNT), because it used the nucleus of a differentiated (somatic) cell. SCNT represented a remarkable advance, and soon after the generation of Dolly, a number of other animals were cloned by SCNT, including pigs, goats, rats, mice, dogs, horses, and mules. The use of SCNT to clone primates has proven more difficult, and in the case of humans, SCNT has been carried out with limited success in embryos.

In 2013 scientists reported the first successful attempt at cloning human embryos with SCNT, specifically for the production of embryonic stem cells (ESCs). By cloning adult cells from a person's body with SCNT, researchers can generate patient-specific ESCs—pluripotent cells that are a perfect genetic match for the patient and that could be used to treat disease. Scientists suspect that compared with ESCs from another individual, patient-specific ESCs may be less likely to be rejected by a patient's body following transplantation.

The use of human embryos to generate ESCs is highly controversial, however, because during the process, the embryo is destroyed. Some people equate that destruction with the loss of a life. Others argue that embryos are not sufficiently advanced to be considered individuals or would have been discarded from fertility or other medical clinics regardless. Putting them to use for science, they argue, is better than allowing them to go to waste entirely.

## A NEW KIND OF STEM CELL

In 2006 Japanese scientist Shinya Yamanaka announced a breakthrough with the potential to lay to rest the debate surrounding the use of human embryos for the generation of ESCs. He had produced so-called induced-pluripotent stem (iPS) cells. The idea for iPS cells was derived from SCNT, the success of which demonstrated that it was possible for differentiated somatic cells to regain pluripotency. Yamanaka sought to induce pluripotency in differentiated cells by genetically modifying them. He accomplished that feat by adding four genes to the nucleus of an adult fibroblast cell from a mouse. The genes effectively reprogrammed the cell, causing it to take on properties similar to those of ESCs.

The realization that the DNA of adult cells could be reprogrammed to a pluripotent state without the use of embryos significantly impacted research into

## SHINYA YAMANAKA

Shinya Yamanaka was born on September 4, 1962, in Ōsaka, Japan. A physician and researcher, Yamanaka developed a revolutionary method for generating stem cells from existing cells of the body. The method involved inserting specific genes into the nuclei of adult cells, a process that resulted in the reversion of cells from an adult state to a pluripotent state. As pluripotent cells, they had regained the capacity to differentiate into any cell type of the body. Thus, the reverted cells became known as induced pluripotent stem (iPS) cells. Yamanaka and British developmental biologist John Bertrand Gurdon shared the 2012 Nobel Prize for Physiology or Medicine for the discovery that mature cells could be reprogrammed.

Yamanaka received an M.D. from Kōbe University in 1987 and a Ph.D. in pharmacology from the Ōsaka City University Graduate School in 1993. That year he joined the Gladstone Institute of Cardiovascular Disease, San Francisco, where he began investigating the *c-Myc* gene in different strains of knockout mice (mice in which a specific gene has been rendered nonfunctional in order to investigate the gene's function). He returned to Ōsaka City University in 1996 and later took a position at the Nara Institute of Science and Technology, where his research became increasingly focused on stem cells. In 2004 he moved to the Institute for Frontier Medical Sciences at Kyōto University, where he began his landmark studies on finding ways to induce pluripotency in cells. He later split his time between Kyōto and the Gladstone Institute of Cardiovascular Disease, becoming a senior investigator at the institute in 2007.

In 2006 Yamanaka announced that he had succeeded in generating iPS cells. The cells had the properties of ESCs but were produced by inserting four specific genes into the nuclei of mouse adult fibroblasts (connective-tissue cells). The following year Yamanaka reported that he had derived iPS cells from human adult fibroblasts—the first successful attempt at generating human versions of these cells. The discovery marked a turning point in stem-cell research, because it offered a way of obtaining human stem cells without the controversial use of human embryos.

Up to that time, Yamanaka's technique to convert adult cells into iPS cells had employed a retrovirus that contained the *c-Myc* gene, which was believed to play a fundamental role in reprogramming adult cell nuclei. However, Yamanaka recognized that the activation of *c-Myc* during the process of creating iPS cells led to the formation of tumours when the stem cells were later transplanted into mice. When he removed the gene from the process, the cells were rendered noncancerous, thereby overcoming a major concern in the therapeutic safety of iPS cells. In 2008 Yamanaka reported another breakthrough—the generation of iPS cells from mouse liver and stomach cells.

Yamanaka received multiple awards for his contributions to stem-cell research, including the Robert Koch Prize (2008), the Shaw Prize in Life Science and Medicine (2008), the Gairdner Foundation International Award (2009), the Albert Lasker Basic Medical Research Award (2009), and the Millennium Technology Prize (2012).

the development of stem cell therapies in medicine. Whereas research with human embryos has been heavily regulated in some countries, significantly slowing progress, work involving the generation of stem cells through genetic reprogramming has advanced at a rapid pace.

Still, many questions remain regarding the extent to which iPS cells are reprogrammed, and their safety and effectiveness for the treatment of disease remains to be tested extensively in clinical trials. For those reasons, and others, some scientists continue to press forward with research on SCNT and ESC production from human embryos.

CHAPTER TWO

# GENE CLONING, DNA ANALYSIS, AND GENE SEQUENCING

Across the biological sciences, gene cloning—the process of making copies of individual genes—is the most common type of cloning carried out by researchers. Along with reproductive and therapeutic cloning, gene cloning represents a type of artificial cloning, but the goals and techniques of gene cloning differ. Recombinant DNA technologies, of which gene cloning is one, entail the artificial manipulation, modification, and recombination of DNA or other nucleic acid molecules. Typically, the technologies are used to modify an organism or population of organisms.

Since the focus of all genetics is the gene, the fundamental goal of laboratory geneticists is to isolate, characterize, and manipulate genes. Although it is relatively easy to isolate a sample of DNA from a collection of cells, finding a specific gene within the DNA sample can be compared to finding a needle in a haystack. Consider the fact that each human cell contains approximately 2 metres (6 feet) of DNA. Therefore, a small tissue sample will contain many kilometres of DNA. However, recombinant DNA technology has made it possible to isolate one gene or any other segment of DNA, enabling researchers to determine its nucleotide sequence, study its transcripts, mutate it in highly specific ways, and reinsert the modified sequence into a living organism.

Recombinant DNA technology has advanced the understanding of many theoretical and practical aspects of gene function and organization. Through recombinant DNA techniques, bacteria have been created that are capable of synthesizing human insulin, human growth hormone, alpha interferon, a hepatitis B vaccine, and other medically useful substances. Plants may be genetically adjusted to enable them to fix nitrogen, and genetic diseases can possibly be corrected by replacing defective genes with normally functioning ones. Thus, the new genetic combinations that are produced through gene cloning are of value to science, medicine, agriculture, or other industries.

## GENE CLONING

In biology a clone is a group of individual cells or organisms descended from one progenitor. Thus, the members of a clone are genetically identical, because cell replication produces identical daughter cells each time.

The use of the word *clone* has been extended to recombinant DNA technology, which has provided scientists with the ability to produce many copies of a single fragment of DNA, such as a gene, creating identical copies that constitute a DNA clone. In practice the procedure is carried out by inserting a DNA fragment into a small DNA molecule and then allowing the molecule to replicate inside a simple living cell such as a bacterium. The small replicating molecule is called a DNA vector (carrier). The most commonly used vectors are plasmids (circular DNA molecules that originated from bacteria), viruses, and yeast cells. Plasmids are not a part of the main cellular genome, but they can carry genes that provide the host cell with useful properties, such as drug resistance, mating ability, and toxin production. They are small enough to be conveniently manipulated experimentally, and, furthermore, they will carry extra DNA that is spliced into them.

## CREATING THE CLONE

The steps in gene cloning are as follows. DNA is extracted from the organism under study and is cut into small fragments of a size suitable for cloning. Most often that is achieved by cleaving the DNA with a restriction enzyme. Restriction enzymes are extracted from several different species and strains of bacteria, in which they act as defense mechanisms against viruses. They can be thought of as "molecular scissors," cutting the DNA at specific target sequences.

The most useful restriction enzymes make staggered cuts. That is, they leave a single-stranded overhang at the site of cleavage. The overhangs are very useful in cloning because the unpaired nucleotides will pair with other overhangs made using the same restriction enzyme. So, if the donor DNA and the vector DNA are both cut with the same enzyme, there is a strong possibility that the donor fragments and the cut vector will splice together because of the complementary overhangs. The resulting molecule is called recombinant DNA. It is recombinant in the sense that it is composed of DNA from two different sources. Thus, it is a type of DNA that would be impossible naturally and is an artifact created by DNA technology.

The next step in the cloning process is to cut the vector with the same restriction enzyme used to cut the donor DNA. Vectors have target sites for many different restriction enzymes, but the most convenient ones are those that occur only once in the vector molecule. That is because the restriction enzyme then merely opens up the vector ring, creating a space for the insertion of the donor DNA segment. Cut vector DNA and donor DNA are mixed in a test tube, and the complementary ends of both types of DNA unite randomly. Several types of unions are possible: donor fragment to donor fragment, vector fragment to vector fragment, and, most important, vector fragment to donor fragment, which can be selected for.

Recombinant DNA associations form spontaneously in the above manner, but the associations are not stable because, although the ends are paired, the sugar-phosphate backbone of the DNA has not been sealed. The latter is accomplished by the application of an enzyme called DNA ligase, which seals the two segments, forming a continuous and stable double helix.

The mixture should now contain a population of vectors, each with a different donor insert. The solution is mixed with live bacterial cells that have been specially treated to make their cells more permeable to DNA. Recombinant molecules enter living cells in a process called transformation. Usually, only a single recombinant molecule will enter any individual bacterial cell. Once inside, the recombinant DNA molecule replicates like any other plasmid DNA molecule, and many copies are subsequently produced. Furthermore, when the bacterial cell divides, all of the daughter cells receive the recombinant plasmid, which again replicates in each daughter cell.

The original mixture of transformed bacterial cells is spread out on the surface of a growth medium in a flat dish (Petri dish) so that the cells are separated from one another. The individual cells are invisible to the naked eye, but as each cell undergoes successive rounds of cell division, visible colonies form. Each colony is a cell clone, but it is also a DNA clone because the recombinant vector has now been amplified by replication during every round of cell division. Thus, the Petri dish, which may contain many hundreds of distinct colonies, represents a large number of clones of different DNA fragments. The collection of clones is called a DNA library. By considering the size of the donor genome and the average size of the inserts in the recombinant DNA molecule, a researcher can calculate the number of clones needed to encompass the entire donor genome, or, in other words, the number of clones needed to constitute a genomic library.

Another type of library is a cDNA library. Creation of a cDNA library begins with messenger ribonucleic acid (mRNA) instead of DNA. Messenger RNA carries encoded information from DNA to ribosomes for translation into protein. To create a cDNA library, the mRNA molecules are treated with the enzyme reverse transcriptase, which is used to make a DNA copy of an mRNA. The resulting DNA molecules are called complementary DNA (cDNA). A cDNA library represents a sampling of the transcribed genes, whereas a genomic library includes untranscribed regions.

Both genomic and cDNA libraries are made without regard to obtaining functional cloned donor fragments. Genomic clones do not necessarily contain full-length copies of genes. Furthermore, genomic DNA from eukaryotes contains introns, which are regions of

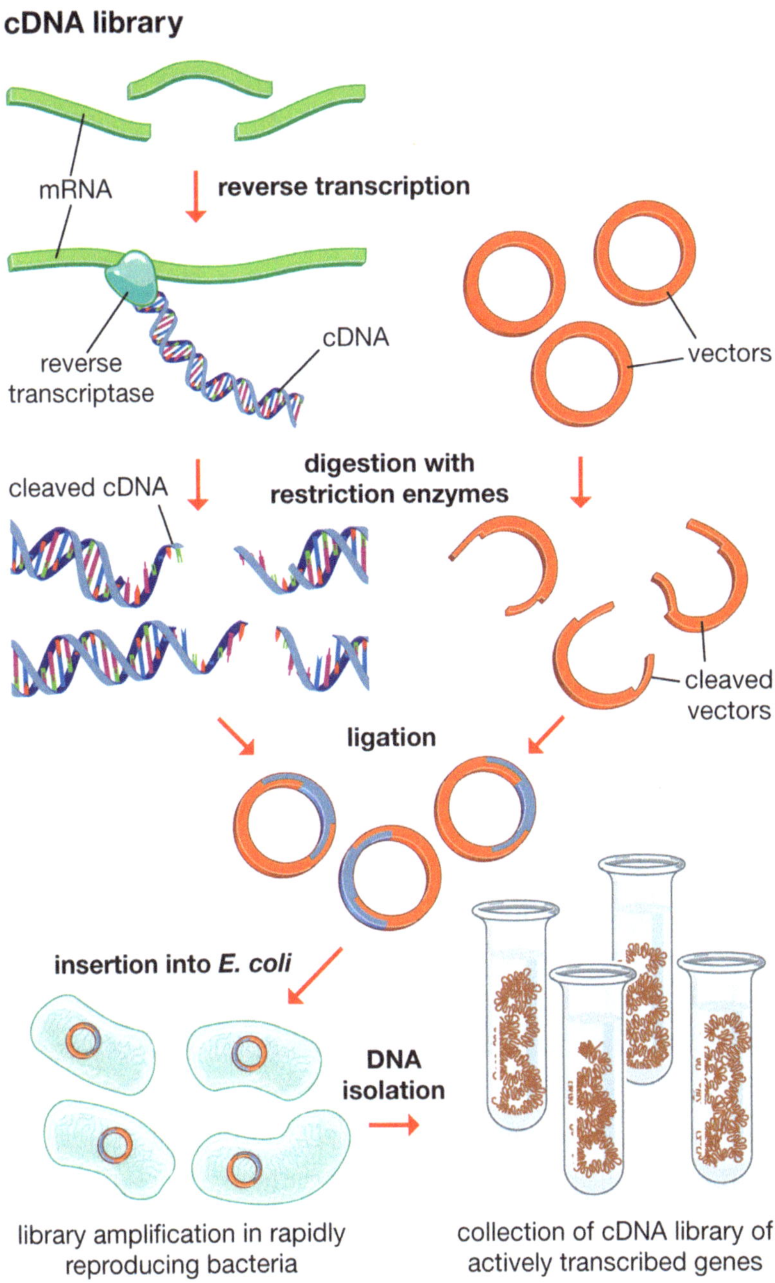


*Complementary DNA (cDNA) is a copy of DNA that is synthesized from messenger RNA (mRNA). It is created through reverse transcription of mRNA. A library of cDNA, which represents only the genes that are encoded into proteins by a genome or region of interest within a genome, is generated using DNA cloning technology.*

DNA that are not translated into protein and cannot be processed by bacterial cells. So, even full-sized genes are not translated in their entirety. In addition, eukaryotic regulatory signals are different from those used by prokaryotes. However, it is possible to produce expression libraries by slicing cDNA inserts immediately adjacent to a bacterial promoter region on the vector. In such expression libraries, eukaryotic proteins are made in bacterial cells, which allows several important technological applications.

Several bacterial viruses have also been used as vectors. The most commonly used is the lambda phage. The central part of the lambda genome is not essential for the virus to replicate in *E. coli*, so it can be excised using an appropriate restriction enzyme, and inserts from donor DNA can be spliced into the gap. In fact, when the phage repackages DNA into its protein capsule, it includes only DNA fragments the same length of the normal phage genome.

Vectors are chosen depending on the total amount of DNA that must be included in a library. Cosmids are engineered vectors that are hybrids of plasmid and phage lambda. However, they can carry larger inserts than either pUC plasmids (plasmids engineered to produce a very high number of DNA copies but that can accommodate only small inserts) or lambda phage alone. Bacterial artificial chromosomes (BACs) are vectors based on F-factor (fertility factor) plasmids of *E. coli* and can carry much larger amounts of DNA. Yeast artificial chromosomes (YACs) are vectors based on autonomously replicating plasmids of *Saccharomyces cerevisiae* (bakers yeast). In yeast (a eukaryotic organism) a YAC behaves like a yeast chromosome and segregates properly into daughter cells. YAC vectors can carry the largest inserts of all and are used extensively in cloning large genomes, such as the human genome.

## ISOLATING THE CLONE

In general, cloning is undertaken to obtain the clone of one particular gene or DNA sequence of interest. The next step after cloning, therefore, is to find and isolate that clone among other members of the library. If the library encompasses the whole genome of an organism, then somewhere within that library will be the desired clone. There are several ways of finding it, depending on the specific gene concerned. Most commonly, a cloned DNA segment that shows homology to the sought gene is used as a probe. For example, if a mouse gene has already been cloned, then that clone can be used to find the equivalent human clone from a human genomic library.

Bacterial colonies constituting a library are grown in a collection of Petri dishes. Then a porous membrane is laid over the surface of each plate, and cells adhere to the membrane. The cells are ruptured, and DNA is separated into single strands all on the membrane. The probe is also separated into single strands and labeled, often with radioactive phosphorus. A solution of the radioactive probe is then used to bathe the membrane. The single-stranded probe DNA will adhere only to the DNA of the clone that contains the equivalent gene. The membrane is dried and placed against a sheet of radiation-sensitive film, and somewhere on the films a black spot will appear, announcing the presence and location of the desired clone. The clone can then be retrieved from the original Petri dishes.

## DNA SEQUENCING

Following cloning, there is often a sufficient amount of genetic material available to deduce the sequence of a chain of nucleotides. An organism's DNA sequence contains all the information needed for its development.

### USES OF DNA SEQUENCING

With information about a DNA sequence, researchers are able to identify and better understand the key elements in an organism's genetic code. Among those elements are genes, which encode the proteins that make up an organism. The identification of genes can be accomplished by searching for known features of genes. Examples of such features include long stretches of DNA known as open reading frames

(ORFs), which are indicative of protein-coding regions. Stretches of DNA that are rich in cytosine and guanine, clusters known as CpG islands, lie close to genes, and so their presence in a DNA sequence can also help researchers locate genes. DNA sequencing can also be used to understand gene function, since certain amino acid sequences are characteristic of certain classes of proteins. Examples include proteins that span cell membranes and thus contain a characteristic transmembrane domain. DNA sequencing also allows for the comparison of genes and other nucleotide sequences of different species. Such comparisons have enabled scientists to better understand evolutionary relationships of species.

## METHODS OF DNA SEQUENCING

DNA sequencing can be carried out with first-generation sequencing technologies or next-generation sequencing technologies. First-generation technologies include the Maxam-Gilbert method and the Sanger method. The Sanger method, which was the most widely used approach, is based on the synthesis of nucleotide chains on a template strand. As the DNA chain is replicated, dideoxy nucleotides are incorporated, thereby stopping chain growth. The dideoxy nucleotides are labeled, either radioactively or fluorescently, enabling researchers to visualize them. The process is carried out for each of the four bases (A, C, T, and G) in DNA.

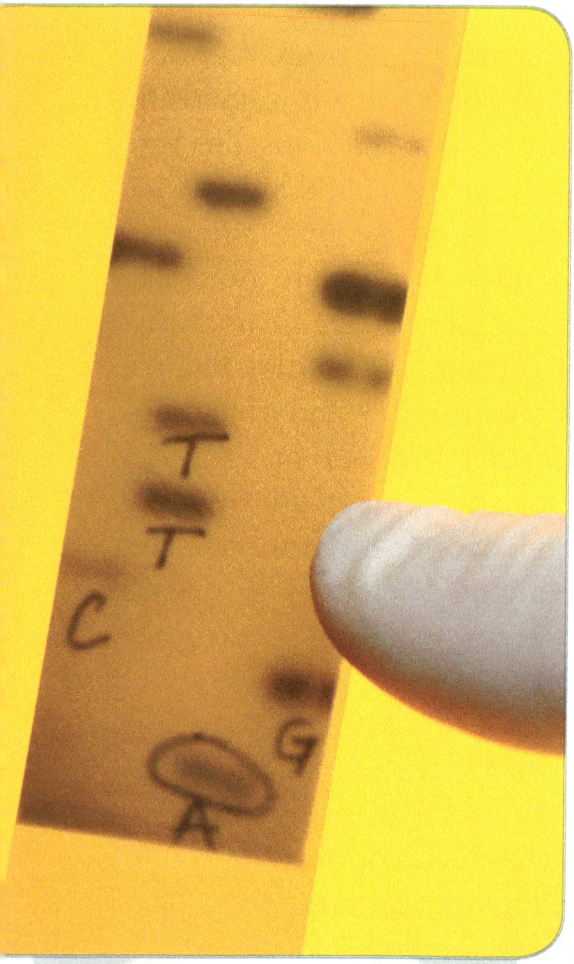


A scientist points to bands that represent nucleotide bases (A, C, T, G) in an X-ray image of a gel. The DNA sequencing method shown here is called the Sanger method. In this particular example, an orange filter was added to the light table to add contrast and help in observing the DNA bands.

Because chain termination occurs when a specific DNA letter is incorporated, researchers are able to assemble the different fragments to deduce the nucleotide sequence.

The Sanger and Maxan-Gilbert methods have been largely supplanted by next-generation sequencing technologies, also known as massively parallel sequencing or second-generation sequencing. The next-generation approaches are automated and are much faster and have significantly greater capacity than first-generation technologies. Millions of DNA fragments can be sequenced at one time with the newer methods. Massive amounts of data are

## PAUL BERG

Paul Berg, born on June 30, 1926, in New York, New York, was an American biochemist whose development of recombinant-DNA techniques won him a share (with Walter Gilbert and Frederick Sanger) of the Nobel Prize for Chemistry in 1980.

After graduating from Pennsylvania State College (later renamed Pennsylvania State University) in 1948 and taking a doctorate from Western Reserve University in 1952, Berg pursued further studies at the Institute of Cytophysiology in Copenhagen and at Washington University in St. Louis, where he remained as assistant professor of microbiology until 1959. From 1959 he was associated with the medical school of Stanford University, serving as chairman of the biochemistry department in 1969–74 and becoming Willson professor (1970) and director of the Beckman Center for Molecular and Genetic Medicine (1985).

In the course of studying the actions of isolated genes, Berg developed methods for splitting DNA molecules at selected sites and attaching segments of the molecule to the DNA of a virus or plasmid, which could then enter bacterial or animal cells. The foreign DNA was incorporated into the host and caused the synthesis of proteins that were not ordinarily found there. One of the earliest practical results of recombinant technology was the development of a strain of bacteria containing the gene for producing the mammalian hormone insulin.

produced through next-generation sequencing, but with advances in bioinformatics, scientists have been able to process and analyze sequencing data with unprecedented speed.

## IN VITRO MUTAGENESIS

Another use of cloned DNA is in vitro mutagenesis, in which a mutation is produced in a segment of cloned DNA. The DNA is then inserted into a cell or organism, and the effects of the mutation are studied. Mutations are useful to geneticists in enabling them to investigate the components of any biological process. However, traditional mutational analysis relied on the occurrence of random spontaneous mutations—a hit-or-miss method in which it was impossible to predict the precise type or position of the mutations obtained. In vitro mutagenesis, however, allows specific mutations to be tailored for type and for position within the gene. A cloned gene is treated in the test tube (in vitro) to obtain the specific mutation desired. The DNA fragment is then reintroduced into the living cell, where it replaces the resident gene. One method of in vitro mutagenesis is oligonucleotide-directed mutagenesis. A specific point in a sequenced gene is pinpointed for mutation. An oligonucleotide, a short stretch of synthetic DNA of the desired sequence, is made chemically. For example, the oligonucleotide might have adenine in one specific location instead of guanine. The oligonucleotide is hybridized to the complementary strand of the cloned gene. It will hybridize despite the one base pair mismatch. Various enzymes are added to allow the oligonucleotide to prime the synthesis of a complete strand within the vector. When the vector is introduced into

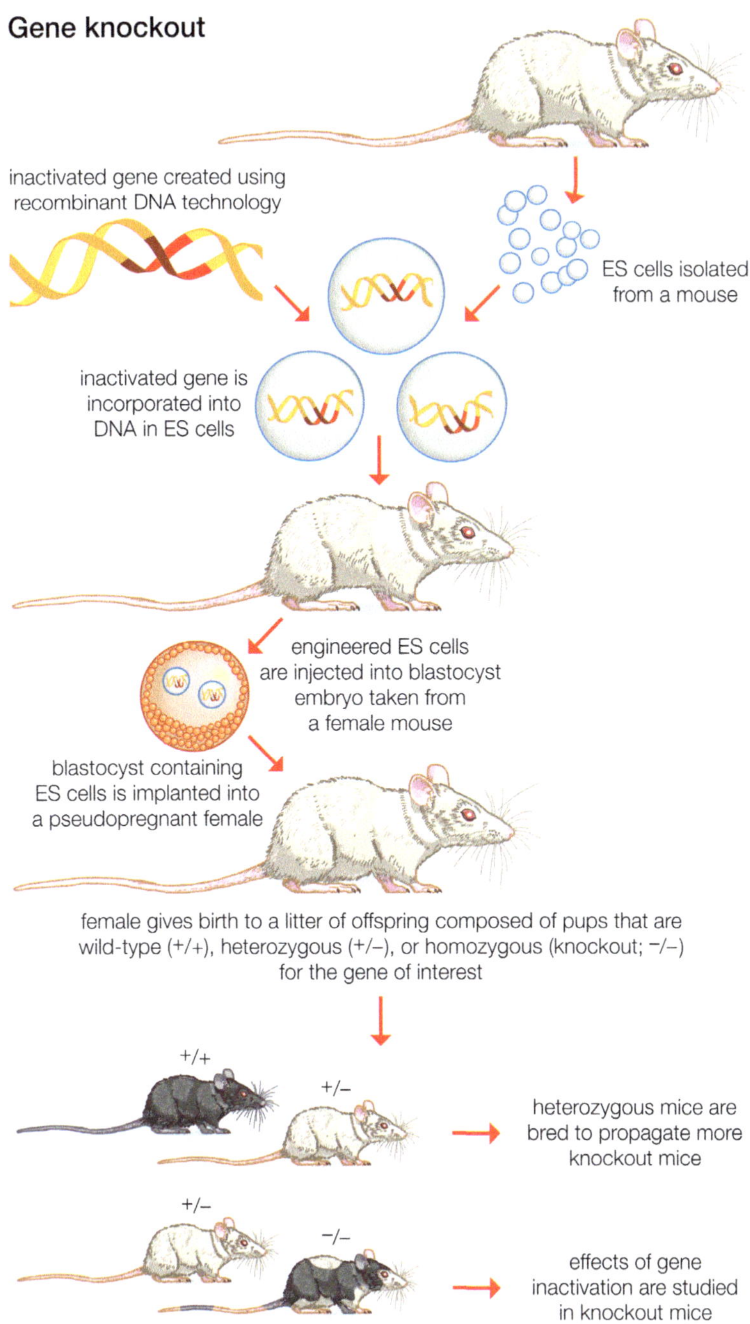


*A version of vitro mutagenesis called gene disruption, or gene knockout, is shown here. A functional gene is replaced by an inactivated gene that is created using recombinant DNA technology. When a gene is "knocked out," the resulting mutant phenotype (observable characteristics) often reveals the gene's biological function.*

a bacterial cell and replicates, the mutated strand will act as a template for a complementary strand that will also be mutant, and thus a fully mutant molecule is obtained. The fully mutant cloned molecule is then reintroduced into the donor organism, and the mutant DNA replaces the resident gene.

Another version of in vitro mutagenesis is gene disruption, or gene knockout. Here, the resident functional gene is replaced by a completely non-functional copy. The advantage of the technique over random mutagenesis is that specific genes can be knocked out at will, leaving all other genes untouched by the mutagenic procedure.

## GENE CLONING AND GENETICALLY MODIFIED ORGANISMS

The ability to obtain specific DNA clones using recombinant DNA technology has made it possible to add the DNA of one organism to the genome of another. The added gene is called a transgene. The transgene inserts itself into a chromosome and is passed to the progeny as a new component of the genome. The resulting organism carrying the transgene is called a transgenic organism or a genetically modified organism (GMO). In that way, a "designer organism" is made that contains some specific change required for an experiment in basic genetics or for improvement of some commercial strain. Multiple transgenic plants have been produced. Genes for toxins

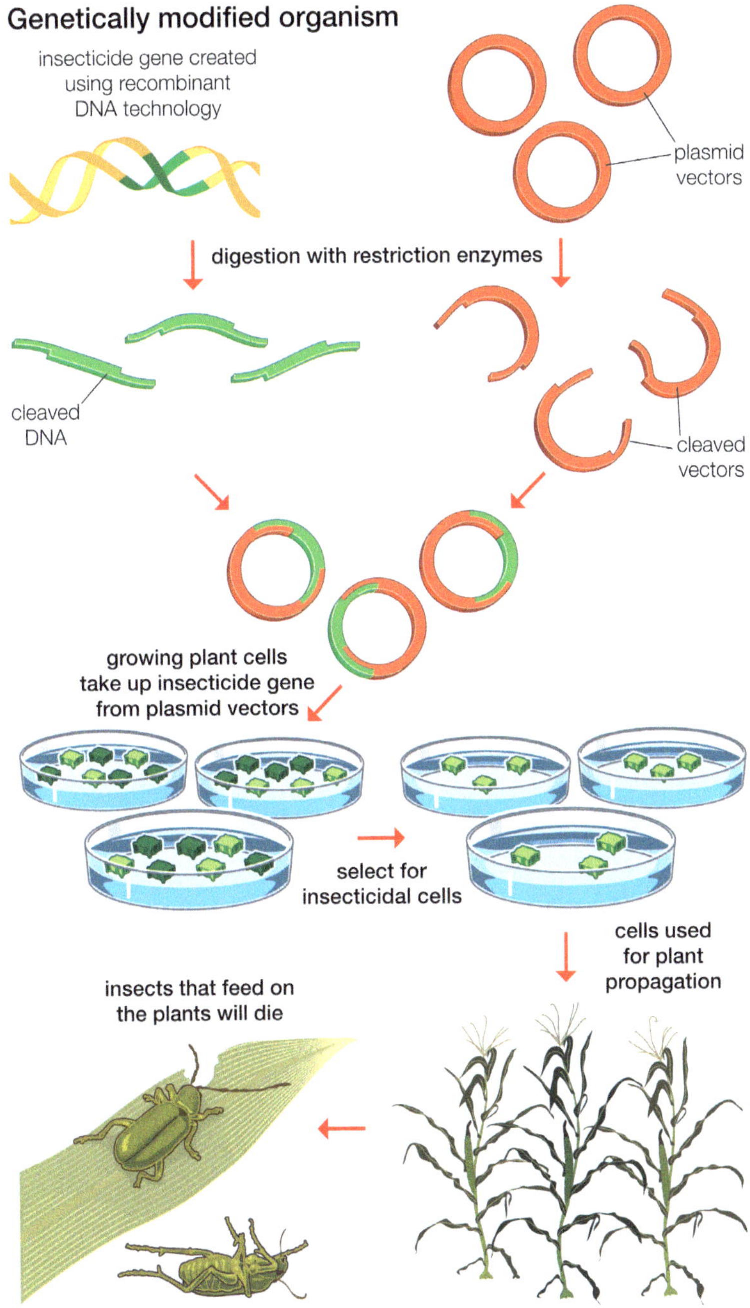


*Genetically modified organisms are produced using scientific methods that include recombinant DNA technology and reproductive cloning. Recombinant DNA technology involves the insertion of one or more individual genes from an organism of one species into the DNA of another.*

that kill insects have been introduced in several species, for example, including corn and cotton. Bacterial genes that confer resistance to herbicides also have been introduced into crop plants. Other plant transgenes aim at improving the nutritional value of the plant.

## REVERSE GENETICS

Recombinant DNA technology has made possible a type of genetics called reverse genetics. Traditionally, genetic research starts with a mutant phenotype, and, by Mendelian crossing analysis, a researcher is able to attribute the phenotype to a specific gene. Reverse genetics travels in precisely the opposite direction. Researchers begin with a gene of unknown function and use molecular analysis to determine its phenotype. One important tool in reverse genetics is gene knockout. By mutating the cloned gene of unknown function and using it to replace the resident copy or copies, the resultant mutant phenotype will show which biological function this gene normally controls.

## DIAGNOSTICS

Recombinant DNA technology has led to powerful diagnostic procedures useful in both medicine and forensics. In medicine such diagnostic procedures are used in counseling prospective parents as to the likelihood of having a child with a particular disease, and they are also used in the prenatal prediction of genetic disease in the fetus. Researchers look for specific DNA fragments that are located in close proximity to the gene that causes the disease of concern. The fragments, called restriction fragment length polymorphisms (RFLPs), often serve as effective genetic markers. In forensics, DNA fragments called variable number tandem repeats (VNTRs), which are highly variable between individuals, are employed to produce what is called a DNA fingerprint. A DNA fingerprint can be used to determine if blood or other body fluids left at the scene of a crime belongs to a suspect.

## PROTEIN MANUFACTURE

Recombinant DNA procedures also have been used to convert bacteria into "factories" for the synthesis of foreign proteins. The technique is useful not only for preparing large amounts of protein for basic research but also for producing valuable proteins for medical use. For example, the genes for human proteins such as growth hormone, insulin, and blood-clotting factor can be commercially manufactured. Another approach to producing proteins via recombinant DNA technology is to introduce the desired gene into the genome of an animal, engineered in such a way that the protein is secreted in the animal's milk, facilitating harvesting.

*Geneticists prepare samples for DNA fingerprinting, a technique used to determine kinship and to solve crimes. DNA fingerprinting originally was based on restriction fragment length polymorphism (RFLP) technology. More recent approaches are based on the use of the polymerase chain reaction (PCR) and so-called microsatellites (or short tandem repeats, STRs).*

## GENOMICS

The full genetic blueprint of an organism is known as its genome, and hence the field of science concerned with better understanding the structure and function of genomes is called genomics. The development of recombinant DNA technology provided the basis for the field of genomics, which in turn has enabled key advances in gene discovery and medicine and in scientific understanding of heredity and evolutionary relationships between species.

Elucidating the sequence of genomic DNA is a central aspect of genomics. In eukaryotes, genomic DNA is housed in the cell nucleus and specifically within the chromosomes in the nucleus. Chromosomes are found in every organism, though their precise number and size varies by species. Within chromosomes are genes, and hence the chromosomes are considered to be the basic units of heredity.

Chromosomes were first described around the middle of the 19th century, but it was not until 1920 that the term *genome* was introduced to describe the complete set of an organism's genetic material. In the 20th century, scientists found that parts of chromosomes could be exchanged through a phenomenon called crossing over, which occurs during the cell division process known as meiosis. By observing the frequency of exchange, researchers were able to determine the distance between genes on the same chromosome and thereby map genes on chromosomes. In general, the mapping of genes by chromosomal crossing over applied almost exclusively to genes that gave rise to observable abnormalities in an organism, or mutant phenotypes. Such mutants comprise only a small fraction of the complete set of genes in an organism's genome. When DNA sequencing and bioinformatics technologies were developed that enabled scientists to elucidate and analyze complete genomic sequences, the field of genomics was born.

## SEQUENCING AND ANALYSIS OF GENOMES

Next-generation sequencing technologies allow for the automated determination of genomic sequences. Such sequencing is carried out in a massively parallel fashion, meaning that millions of sequencing reactions, to analyze millions of DNA fragments, are performed at one time. To accomplish that feat, genomic DNA is first cut into fragments, forming what is known as a genomic library. The fragments are then sequenced across millions of reactions in parallel. The reads, or newly sequenced chains, are then put back together, being reassembled de novo (from scratch) or according to a known reference genome. Once aligned, the reads collectively make up the complete chromosomal sequence in the sample of genomic DNA.

## GENOMICS APPLICATIONS

Genomics has numerous applications, including in the determination of gene function, an area known generally as functional genomics. Gene function can be determined in several ways, including with classical, or forward, genetic methodology. Such classical methodology begins with a mutant phenotype of interest, obtained at random. The mutant is then used to identify the sequence and function of the normal gene. In reverse genetics, the normal gene sequence is first determined through genomics. A targeted mutation is then introduced into the gene. Observation of how the mutation affects phenotype provides information on the normal function of the gene. Forward and reverse genetics are complementary. A gene discovered using forward methodology that has been mapped to a specific location on a chromosome may already have an annotated function that has been described through reverse genetics

Genomics is also used to identify complete subsets of genes that are involved in temporal or developmental events of an organism, for example. Microarray technology allows a sample of cloned DNA for each gene in a whole genome to be arranged in order on the surface of a thin piece of glass. The glass, which is a sort of chip, is treated to encourage DNA molecules to stick to its surface. For any phenomenon of interest, such as a specific developmental stage (e.g., limb bud growth in an animal), the total RNA is extracted from the organism's cells, labeled with a special dye that fluoresces, and applied to the surface of a microarray chip. Through base pairing, the RNAs are the sample bind to the genes from which they were originally transcribed. Their attachment results in fluorescent emissions on the chip's surface, thereby enabling the full set of genes that were transcribed during the biological phenomenon of interest to be identified. Through the assembly of the subset of genes involved in a biological process, forward genetics can be used to achieve the same goal. Forward genetics begins with the induction of mutations with phenotypes that appear to change the biological process of interest. That step it followed by work to identify the genes that normally guide the process. Forward genetics is limited, however, in that is can be used only to find genes with mutations that result in readily observable mutant phenotypes. Genes with mutations that produce subtle changes can be easily missed.

Through classical genetics methodologies, researchers have been able to make fascinating discoveries about evolutionary relationships between organisms and species. In the past, comparisons of chromosome size, number, and banding patterns were made primarily with classical approaches, which provided valuable information about relationships between populations, species, and genera.

With entire genomic sequences, however, scientists have been able to carry out such comparisons at remarkable depth, owing to the significantly greater resolving power of comparative genomics relative to classical genetics. Comparative genomics also has great sensitivity and can be used on small scales, which allows for the detection of subtle differences between sequences.

Examples of applications of comparative genomics include the study of evolutionary relationships between humans and chimpanzees, which have been shown to possess high levels of genomic similarity. In the case of different populations of humans, comparative genomics has revealed that the human species is a genetic continuum. Differences between human populations are limited to only a small subset of genes that influence superficial factors, including skin colour. Degrees of relatedness between organisms can be analyzed through the mathematical measurement of DNA sequences.

CHAPTER THREE

# AN OVERVIEW OF ANIMAL AND PLANT REPRODUCTION PROCESSES

The scientific techniques and applications of cloning are sophisticated, and they are modern, with their development originating in the 20th century. But cloning is not a new concept in nature. Throughout the evolutionary history of animals and plants, many lower, or less complex, species have depended on reproductive processes that essentially produce offspring that are clones of the parent organism. Even some relatively more complex, or more highly evolved, species reproduce asexually, thereby producing clones. Among animals, higher, or more complex, species have relied almost exclusively on sexual reproduction, in which a new individual is produced through the recombination of genetic material from sperm and egg.

Asexual reproduction is an efficient means of reproduction. But in the context of adaptation and natural selection, it is not especially advantageous. Indeed, asexually reproducing populations are, for the most part, genetically fixed. Potentially harmful mutations that exist within a population are allowed to persist. So long as their environment remains stable, asexually reproducing organisms can thrive. When their environment changes, however, an entire population may go extinct. By contrast, sexual reproduction encourages genetic diversification, rather than duplication. By testing novel genetic combinations, sexually reproducing species are able to hone their adaptation to their environments and respond to changing conditions. Through the recombination of genes, sexual reproduction also offers a mechanism whereby harmful mutations can be eliminated from a population.

The risks and rewards of asexual and sexual reproductive strategies are relevant to the science of cloning. The production of genetic duplicates of animals, for example, has consequences for those individual animals. Many are unable to reproduce. Likewise, the propagation of populations of genetically identical plants, such as on fruit orchards, may have impacts on the ability of those populations to respond to environmental change. To understand those impacts, a knowledge of the many different processes of reproduction that exist in nature is critical. Through knowing the natural mechanisms of reproduction, scientists are better able to understand and apply cloning technologies.

## REPRODUCTIVE SYSTEMS OF INVERTEBRATES

Although asexual reproduction occurs in many invertebrate species, most actually reproduce sexually. The basic unit of sexual reproduction is a gamete, produced by the specialized tissues of the gonads. Sexual reproduction does not necessarily imply copulation or even a union of gametes.

As might be expected of such a large and diverse group as the invertebrates, many variations have evolved to ensure the survival of species. Some invertebrates have coexistent female and male gonads, whereas in others the same gonad produces both sperm and eggs. Animals in which both sperm and eggs are produced by the same individual (hermaphroditism) are described as monoecious. In dioecious species, the sexes are separate. Generally, the male gonads ripen first in hermaphroditic animals (a phenomenon known as protandry), which tends to ensure cross-fertilization. Self-fertilization is normal, however, in many species, and some species even undergo sex reversal. A number of free-living nematodes, for example, are capable of sex reversal—if the sex ratio in a given population is not optimal or if environmental conditions are not ideal, the ratio of males to females can be altered.

*These earthworms* (Lumbricus terrestris) *are mating. An earthworm is an invertebrate and is hermaphroditic. Its functional reproductive organs occur in the same individual but it does not self-fertilize—the eggs of one individual are fertilized by the sperm of another. After mating, the worms separate and form cocoons, which pick up eggs at the 14th segment and sperm at the 9th and 10th segments. The cocoon is deposited in the soil and within two to four weeks, tiny earthworms emerge.*

## REPRODUCTIVE SYSTEMS OF VERTEBRATES

The reproductive organs of vertebrates consist of gonads and associated ducts and glands. In addition, some vertebrates, including some of the more primitive fishes, have organs for sperm transfer or oviposition (egg-laying). Gonads produce the gametes

## PARTHENOGENESIS

Parthenogenesis is a remarkable reproductive strategy. Most frequently, it entails the development of a new individual from an unfertilized gamete. Often referred to as unisexual reproduction, it has been observed in almost every major invertebrate group and frequently occurs alternately with bisexual reproduction (reproduction by union of gametes). Some species, in which males are completely unknown, apparently reproduce only by parthenogenesis. Species that alternate between parthenogenesis and bisexual reproduction (heterogenetic species) often do so in response to changes in population density, food availability, or other environmental conditions.

The best-known examples of parthenogenetic reproduction are found among rotifers. Males are completely unknown in some genera. In others, they appear in the population only for brief periods and more or less seasonally. Females are the dominant form or are the only sex present in a population throughout most of the year. Because no reductional division (meiosis) occurs in the course of egg maturation, the eggs are diploid—they have the full number of chromosomes, such that they give rise to new diploid individuals with no chromosomal contribution from a male gamete.

In certain species of arthropods, such as water fleas, so long as environmental conditions are optimal and food is plentiful, females produce other females by parthenogenesis. When conditions become adverse, males begin to appear in the population, and bisexual reproduction follows.

Insects provide numerous examples of parthenogenesis of varying degrees of complexity. One of the most notable is that of the honeybee. Unfertilized eggs develop into drones, which are males. Fertilized eggs become worker females, which are kept in a non-reproductive state by secretions from the reproductive female, the queen bee.

Life cycles involving alternation between parthenogenesis and bisexual reproduction can be found in many species of flies. Aphids, for example, have a seasonal cycle consisting of a bisexual winter phase and a parthenogenetic summer phase. Temperature change, length of day, and food availability play major roles in initiating the phases.

and hormones essential for reproduction. Associated ducts and glands store and transport the gametes and secrete necessary substances. In addition to those structures, most male and female vertebrates have a cloaca, a cavity that serves as a common terminal chamber for the digestive, urinary, and reproductive tracts and empties to the outside.

Among lower vertebrates, mature gonads sometimes produce both sperm and eggs. In fishes, for example, hermaphroditism is more general in cyclostomes and teleosts than in other species. A teleost may function as a male during the early part of its sexual life and as a female later. Hermaphroditism is uncommon among amphibians, although it frequently occurs as an anomaly. In vertebrates above amphibians, true hermaphroditism probably does not exist.

## THE TESTES

In males, the testes, a paired organ, produces sperm. Testes in vertebrates below mammals and in certain groups of mammals, such as monotremes and cetaceans, lie within the body. In humans the testes occur as a pair of oval-shaped organs that are contained within a scrotal sac, a pouch located directly behind the penis.

The testes contain supporting cells called Sertoli cells, and testosterone-producing cells called Leydig (interstitial) cells. Leydig cells are present in most, if not all, male vertebrates. They are not always readily distinguishable, however. In some bird species, for example, they may be seen only with the electron microscope.

Within the testes are coiled tubules, known as the seminiferous tubules, in which the sperm are produced. In human males, the seminiferous tubules constitute about 90 percent of the testicular mass. In the young male the tubules are simple and composed of undeveloped sperm-producing cells (spermatogonia) and the Sertoli cells. In the older male the tubules become branched, and spermatogonia are changed into the fertile sperm cells after a series of transformations called spermatogenesis. The Sertoli cells found in both young and adult males mechanically support and protect the spermatogonia.

Each seminiferous tubule of the adult testis has a central lumen, or cavity, which is connected to the epididymis and spermatic duct (ductus deferens). Sperm cells originate as spermatogonia along the walls of the seminiferous tubules. The spermatogonia mature into spermatocytes, which mature into spermatids that mature into spermatozoa as they move into the central lumen of the seminiferous tubule. The spermatozoa migrate, by short contractions of the tubule, to the mediastinum testis. They are then transported through a complex network of canals (rete testis and efferent ductules) to the epididymis for temporary storage. The spermatozoa move through the epididymis and the spermatic duct to be stored in the seminal vesicles for eventual ejaculation with the seminal fluid.

## THE OVARIES

The ovaries are the vertebrate female reproductive organs in which sex cells (eggs, or ova) are produced. They lie within the body cavity but have variable form among the vertebrates. Their appearance depends on many factors, including whether one egg or thousands are discharged (ovulated), whether the eggs are immature or ripe, and whether mature eggs are small or large. The season of the year in seasonal breeders (the ovary enlarges during breeding seasons, diminishes in size between seasons) and the age of the animal (whether juvenile, reproductively active, or past reproductive age) are other factors affecting the form of the ovaries.

Structurally, a typical vertebrate ovary consists of a cortex and medulla. The cortex contains future eggs and, at one time or another, developing eggs. It undergoes fluctuations in size and appearance that correlate with stages of the reproductive cycle. The cortex also contains remnants of ovulated follicles and, in mammals, clusters of interstitial cells. The cortical components are embedded in a supportive framework of connective, vascular, and neural tissue that constitutes the stroma. The medulla lies internal to the cortex and consists of blood and lymph vessels, nerves, and connective tissue.

An ovarian follicle consists of an oocyte, or immature egg, surrounded by an epithelium, the cells of which are referred to as follicular or granulosa cells. The primitive role of the follicular cells appears to be the secretion of the yolk-forming material onto or into the oocyte. Follicular cells may also have a role in converting substances produced elsewhere in the body into female hormones, or estrogens.

Mammalian follicles above monotremes are unique in that they develop a fluid-filled cavity (antrum) within the granulosa layer. During antrum formation, cell division of the granulosa cells increases, and fluid-filled spaces develop among the cells. The spaces coalesce to form the antrum. Under the influence of pituitary gonadotropic hormones, many antral follicles thereafter continue to grow, forming large so-called Graafian follicles—less than 400 micrometres (μm; about 0.16 inch) in diameter in large mammals and about 150–200 μm (0.006-0.008 inch) in small ones. Graafian follicles contain mature eggs and appear as large blisters on the ovary. In all vertebrates, oocytes that have begun to grow and mature may, at any time until just before ovulation, cease development and undergo atresia, or degeneration. Atresia is a normal process that reduces the number of eggs ovulated.

## OVULATION

The release of a mature egg from the female ovary is known as ovulation. Ovulation enables the egg to be fertilized by male sperm cells. Prior to eruption from the ovary, an egg first must grow and mature. Until stimulated to grow, the primary egg cell passes through a period of dormancy that, in humans, may last several years.

Once a follicle reaches the surface of the ovary, the follicular wall thins. Pressure caused by the follicle and fluid against the ovary's surface causes bulging of the ovarian wall. When the follicle ruptures, the egg and fluid are released along with some torn patches of tissue. In humans, the cells, fluid, and egg are directed

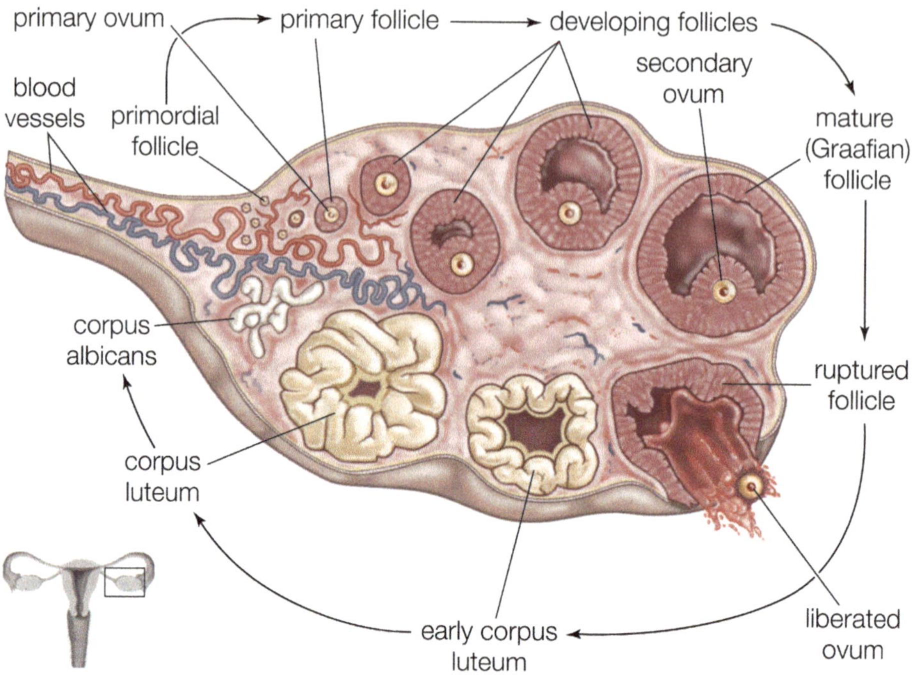


*The steps of ovulation are depicted in this illustration of a human ovary. The process begins with a dormant primordial follicle that grows and matures. The follicle eventually is released from the ovary into the fallopian tube.*

into the nearby fallopian tube, which serves as a passageway by which the egg reaches the uterus and as a site for fertilization of the released egg by sperm.

The hormones that stimulate ovulation are produced in the pituitary gland. In humans, they are known as follicle-stimulating hormone and luteinizing hormone. After the egg leaves the ovary, the walls of the follicle again close, and the space that was occupied by the egg begins to fill with new cells known as the corpus luteum. The corpus luteum secretes the female hormone progesterone, which helps to keep the uterine wall receptive to a fertilized egg. If the egg is not fertilized, the corpus luteum stops secreting progesterone about nine days after ovulation. If the egg becomes fertilized, progesterone continues to be secreted, first by the corpus luteum and then by the placenta, until the child is born. Progesterone blocks the release of more hormones from the pituitary gland, so that further ovulation does not normally occur during pregnancy.

## REPRODUCTION IN PLANTS

In plants, as in animals, the end result of reproduction is the continuation of a given species, and the ability to reproduce is, therefore, rather conservative, or given to only moderate change, during evolution. Changes have occurred, however, and the pattern is demonstrable through a survey of plant groups.

Reproduction in plants is either asexual or sexual. Asexual reproduction in plants involves a variety of widely disparate methods for producing new plants identical in every respect to the parent. Sexual reproduction, on the other hand, depends on a complex series of basic cellular events, involving chromosomes and their genes, that take place within an elaborate sexual apparatus evolved precisely for the development of

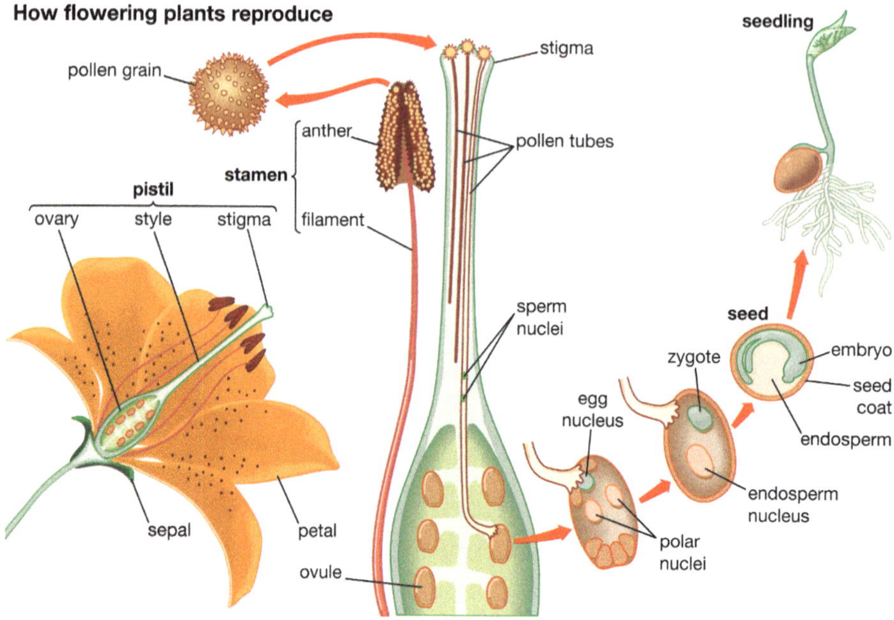


*Reproduction in flowering plants begins with pollination, the transfer of pollen from anther to stigma on the same flower or to the stigma of another flower on the same plant (self-pollination), or from the anther on one plant to the stigma of another plant (cross-pollination). Once the pollen grain lodges on the stigma, a pollen tube grows from the pollen grain to an ovule. Two sperm nuclei then pass through the pollen tube. One of them unites with the egg nucleus and produces a zygote; the other sperm nucleus unites with two polar nuclei to produce an endosperm nucleus. The fertilized ovule develops into a seed.*

new plants in some respects different from the two parents that played a role in their production.

Asexual reproduction involves no union of cells or nuclei of cells and, therefore, no mingling of genetic traits, since the nucleus contains the genetic material of the cell. Systems of asexual reproduction fall into two basic types: systems that utilize almost any fragment or part of a plant body and systems that depend upon specialized structures that have evolved as reproductive agents. In many plant groups, for example, fragmentation of the plant body is followed by regeneration and development of the fragments into whole new organisms. An example of a specialized structure that may be used is an airborne spore, which is seen among mosses, liverworts, and ferns. Such spores are asexual in the sense that they may grow directly into new individuals, without prior sexual union. Specially organized buds, or gemmae, may also serve as agents of asexual reproduction.

The vegetative, or somatic, organs of plants may, in their entirety, be modified to serve as organs of reproduction. Examples include stolons, rhizomes, tubers, corms, and bulbs, as well as the tubers of liverworts, ferns, and horsetails, the dormant buds of certain moss stages, and the leaves of many succulents. Stolons are elongated runners, or horizontal stems, such as those of the strawberry, which root and form new plantlets when they make proper contact with a moist soil surface. Rhizomes, as seen in iris, are fleshy, elongated, horizontal stems that grow within or upon the soil. The branching of rhizomes results in multiplication of the plant. The enlarged fleshy tips of subterranean rhizomes or stolons are known as tubers, examples of which are potatoes. Tubers are fleshy storage stems, the buds ("eyes") of which, under proper conditions, can develop into new individuals. Erect, vertical, fleshy, subterranean stems, which are known as corms, are exemplified by crocuses and gladioli. Those organs tide the plants over periods of dormancy and may develop secondary cormlets, which give rise to new plantlets. Unlike the corm, only a small portion of the bulb, as in lilies and the onion, represents stem tissue. The latter is surrounded by the fleshy food-storage bases of earlier-formed leaves. After a period of dormancy, bulbs develop into new individuals. Large bulbs produce secondary bulbs through the development of buds, resulting in an increase in number of individuals.

In most plant groups, both sexual and asexual methods of reproduction occur. Individual plants may be either bisexual (hermaphroditic), in which male and female gametes are produced by the same organism, or unisexual, producing either male or female gametes but not both. A bisexual individual, however, is not necessarily capable of fertilizing its own eggs. In certain ferns, for example, male gametes of one individual are not compatible with the female gametes of the same individual, so cross-fertilization (with another individual of the species) is obligatory.

Among the liverworts, mosses, and vascular plants, the life cycle involves two different phases, often called generations, although only one plant generation is, in fact, involved in one complete cycle. That type of life cycle is often said to illustrate the "alternation of generations," in which a haploid individual, or tissue, called a gametophyte, at maturity produces gametes that unite in pairs to form diploid zygotes. The latter develop directly into individuals, or tissues, called sporophytes, in which the nuclei of certain fertile cells, called spore mother cells, or sporocytes, give rise to haploid spores. The spores are lightweight and are borne by air currents. They germinate to form the haploid, sexual, gamete-producing phase, usually designated the gametophyte.

## EARLY DEVELOPMENT AND CELL DIFFERENTIATION

Following fertilization, embryological development begins. The differentiation of embryonic tissues proceeds rapidly, particularly during the early course of development. The tissues that will become adult structures—the stems, flowers, or leaves of plants and the limbs, the skin, and all the other parts of an animal—are laid down. In general, the simpler the overall organization of the plant or animal, the fewer the number of distinct cell types that they possess. Mammals contain more than 200 different cell types, whereas simple invertebrate animals may have only a few different types.

It is thought that all of an organism's genes are present in each cell nucleus, no matter what the cell type, and that differences between tissues are not due to the presence or absence of certain genes but are due to the expression of some and the repression of others. In animals the best evidence for retention of the entire set of genes comes from whole animal cloning experiments in which the nucleus of a differentiated cell is substituted for the nucleus of a fertilized egg. In many species that process results in the development of a normal embryo that contains the full range of body parts and cell types. Likewise, in plants it is often possible to grow complete embryos from individual cells in tissue culture. Such experiments show that any nucleus has the genetic information required for the growth of a developing organism, and they strongly suggest that, for most tissues, cell differentiation arises from the regulation of genetic activity rather than the removal or destruction of unwanted genes.

Fully differentiated cells are qualitatively different from one another. States of terminal differentiation are stable and persistent, both in the lifetime of the cell and in successive cell generations. The inherent stability of the differentiated state is maintained by various processes, including feedback activation of genes by their own products and repression of inactive genes.

Differentiation from visibly undifferentiated precursor cells occurs during embryonic development, during metamorphosis of larval forms, and following the separation of parts in asexual reproduction. It also takes place in adult organisms during the renewal of tissues and the regeneration of missing parts. Thus, cell differentiation is an essential and ongoing process at all stages of life.

The visible differentiation of cells is only the last of a progressive sequence of states. In each state, the cell becomes increasingly committed toward one type of cell into which it can develop. States of commitment are sometimes described as "specification" to represent a reversible type of commitment and as "determination" to represent an irreversible commitment. Although states of specification and determination both represent differential gene activity, the properties of embryonic cells are not necessarily the same as those of fully differentiated cells. In particular, cells in specification states are usually not stable over prolonged periods of time.

Two mechanisms bring about altered commitments in the different regions of the early embryo: cytoplasmic localization and induction. Cytoplasmic localization is evident in the earliest stages of development of the embryo. During this time, the embryo divides without growth, undergoing cleavage divisions that produce separate cells called blastomeres. Each blastomere inherits a certain

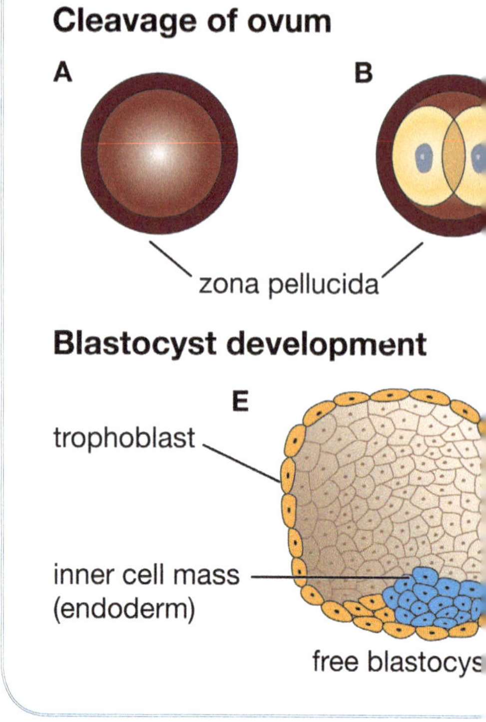


region of the original egg cytoplasm, which may contain one or more regulatory substances called cytoplasmic determinants. When the embryo has become a solid mass of blastomeres (called a morula), it generally consists of two or more differently committed cell populations—a result of the blastomeres having incorporated different cytoplasmic determinants. Cytoplasmic determinants may consist of mRNA or protein in a particular state of activation.

In induction, the second mechanism of commitment, a substance secreted by one group of cells alters the development of another group. In early development, induction is usually instructive; that is, the tissue assumes a different state of commitment in the presence of the signal than it would in the absence of the signal. Inductive signals often take the form of concentration gradients of substances that evoke a number of different responses at different concentrations.

The final stage of differentiation often involves the formation of several types of differentiated cells from one precursor or stem cell population. Terminal

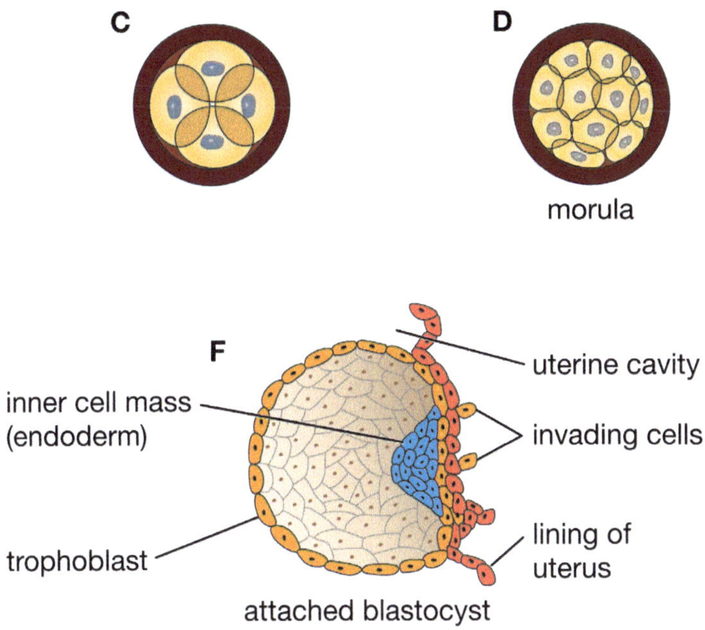


*This illustration depicts the processes of development and cell determination for a human embryo. The ovum contains a small collection of cells in the early stages of human development. As cells divide (A–D), they are separated into different regions of the ovum. Each region of the ovum transmits a unique set of chemical signals to nearby cells. Thus, the signals detected by one cell differ from those detected by its neighbour cells. In this process, known as cell determination, cells are individually programmed to direct them toward development into different cell types.*

differentiation occurs not only in embryonic development but also in many tissues in postnatal life. Control of the process depends on a system of lateral inhibition in which cells that are differentiating along a particular pathway send out signals that repress similar differentiation by their neighbours.

CHAPTER FOUR

# REPRODUCTIVE CLONING AND GENETIC ENGINEERING

Among mammals, naturally occurring clones are rare, existing only in the case of identical siblings, which are derived from a single zygote. But identical siblings are clones of one another—they are not, in other words, clones of a parent. In fact, among mammals, there is no known natural mechanism that results in the production of offspring that are genetically identical to a parent.

Despite that fact, humans have long worked to breed animals in ways that ultimately are intended to reproduce desired traits. Farmers, for example, breed animals that possess superior qualities, such as high milk or egg production. The idea in doing so is simply that the mating of such animals allows for the development and maintenance of populations of animals that are relatively uniform with regard to human-desired traits. But the process is far from perfect. Indeed, only through reproductive cloning is it possible to produce animals that possess precisely the same traits as an already grown individual of the same species.

Reproductive cloning involves the implantation of a cloned embryo into a real or an artificial uterus. The embryo develops into a fetus that is then carried to term. Reproductive cloning experiments initially were performed through the process of embryo splitting, in which a single early-stage two-cell embryo is manually divided into two individual cells and then grows as two identical embryos. But with the birth of Dolly in 1996, there emerged the process of somatic cell nuclear transfer (SCNT).

Reproductive cloning technology has since found potential applications beyond the production of livestock, particularly when combined with the tools of genetic engineering. Nuclear transfer technology is especially powerful in that regard, having numerous possible applications. Genetically modified clones of animals could be used, for example, in the production of pharmaceuticals or in the generation of tissues or organs that could be used for xenotransplantation—the transplantation of animal tissues into humans.

## DOLLY, THE FIRST CLONE OF AN ADULT MAMMAL

Dolly, a Finn Dorset sheep and the first adult mammalian clone, was produced by British developmental biologist Ian Wilmut and colleagues of the Roslin Institute, near Edinburgh, Scotland. The announcement in February 1997 of Dolly's birth marked a milestone in science, dispelling decades of presumption that adult mammals could not be cloned and igniting a debate concerning the many possible uses and misuses of mammalian cloning technology.

The concept of mammalian clones, even humans, was not completely new at the time of Dolly's birth.

*Dolly* (right), *the first sheep that was produced by nuclear transfer from differentiated adult sheep cells, and Polly, the first transgenic lamb that was cloned with an added human gene, are seen here in 1997 in their pen at the Roslin Institute in Edinburgh, Scotland. Polly had a human gene added to her DNA so that her milk contained a blood clotting protein that could be extracted and used in the treatment of hemophilia, a blood disease in humans.*

Among mammals, naturally occurring genetic clones had long been recognized in the form of monozygotic (identical) twins. Unlike Dolly, however, such clones are derived from a single zygote, and thus they are clones of one another, rather than clones of another individual. Moreover, clones had been generated previously in the laboratory, but only from embryonic cells that were either undifferentiated or only partially differentiated. In animals, the production of clones from fully differentiated (adult) cells, such as skin or muscle cells, had been carried out successfully only in lower species, such as frogs.

For decades, scientists had tried and failed to clone mammals from existing adults. The repeated failures led scientists to speculate about the significance of the timing and process of cell differentiation in the developing mammalian embryo. Of particular interest were changes that occurred to DNA during an animal's development, whereby patterns in gene expression were altered as cells became increasingly specialized in function. It was realized that through the process of differentiation, adult mammalian cells lose totipotency, or the ability to become any of the different cell types required for making a complete and viable animal. It was presumed that the process was irreversible. The successful production of Dolly, however, proved otherwise.

Dolly was cloned from a mammary gland cell taken from an adult Finn Dorset ewe. Wilmut and his team of researchers at Roslin created her by using electrical pulses to fuse the mammary cell with an unfertilized egg cell, the nucleus of which had been removed. The fusion process resulted in the transfer of the mammary cell nucleus into the egg cell, which then began to divide. In order for the mammary cell nucleus to be accepted and functional within the host egg, the cell first had to be induced to abandon the normal cycle of growth and division and enter a quiescent stage. To accomplish that, researchers deliberately withheld nutrients from the cells. The importance of the step had been determined experimentally, though an explanation for its necessity was lacking. Nevertheless, starting with a collection of mammary cell nuclei and host egg cytoplasms derived from Scottish Blackface ewes, a number of fused couplets successfully formed embryos. The reconstructed embryos were transferred to surrogate Scottish Blackface ewes. Of thirteen recipient ewes, one became pregnant, and 148 days later, which is essentially normal gestation for a sheep, Dolly was born.

Dolly remained alive and well long after her birth, with a functional heart, liver, brain, and other organs, all derived genetically from the nuclear DNA of an adult mammary gland cell. She was euthanized by veterinarians on Feb. 14, 2003, after being found to suffer from progressive lung disease. Her body was preserved and displayed at the National Museum of Scotland in Edinburgh.

The technique used to produce Dolly essentially was SCNT. SCNT has since been used to generate a wide variety of mammalian clones, from different types of adult cells. Its success in producing clones of primates, however, has been notably limited.

## SOMATIC CELL NUCLEAR TRANSFER

The SCNT technology behind the production of Dolly and, later, other animals entails the removal of the entire nucleus from a somatic (body) cell of an organism, followed by insertion of the nucleus into an egg cell that has had its own nucleus removed (enucleation). Once the somatic nucleus is inside the egg, the egg typically is stimulated with a mild electrical current, after which it begins to divide. Thus, a cloned embryo, essentially an embryo of an identical twin of the original organism, is created.

The SCNT process has undergone significant refinement since the 1990s, and procedures have been developed to prevent damage to eggs during nuclear extraction and somatic cell nuclear insertion. For example, the use of polarized light to visualize an egg cell's nucleus facilitates the extraction of the nucleus from the egg, resulting in a healthy, viable egg and thereby increasing the success rate of SCNT.

While a practical application of SCNT is in the reproductive cloning of farm animals that have

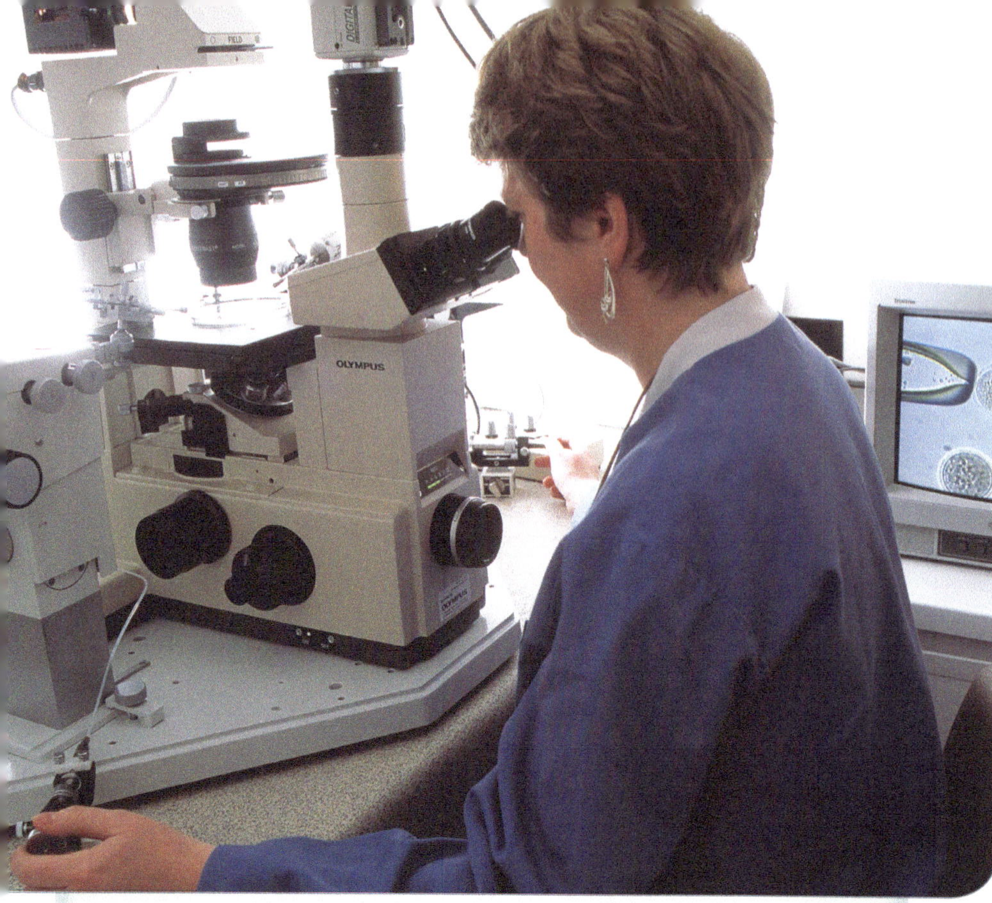

*A technician uses a light microscope to carry out nuclear transfer on a mouse egg. Its genetic material has been removed and an adult cell nucleus is being injected in its place with a needle. The resulting embryo will consist of embryonic stem cells (ESCs).*

exceptional qualities, the technique can be used for different purposes. Most often, the egg is allowed to develop to the blastocyst stage, at which point a culture of embryonic stem cells (ESCs) can be created from the inner cell mass of the blastocyst. Mouse, monkey, and human ESCs have been made using SCNT. Human ESCs have potential applications in both medicine and research. The technique also could be

## FROZEN ARK

In 1996, in response to anticipated, drastic losses in wildlife habitat associated with the growth and rising environmental demands of human populations, an international team of researchers, initially supported by the Natural History Museum, the Zoological Society of London, and the University of Nottingham in the United Kingdom, established the Frozen Ark—a bank of frozen cells and tissue samples to preserve the genetic material of endangered species. Cells and tissues, when prepared carefully for storage at freezing temperatures, can be kept for long periods of time, potentially many decades or even centuries. Among the first species stored in the ark were the scimitar oryx (*Oryx dammah*) and the yellow seahorse (*Hippocampus kuda*).

The Frozen Ark entailed the collection of genetic material from threatened, endangered, and extinct species of animals. Possible sources of such material included blood cells, hairs or feathers, and feces. Samples were stored in liquid nitrogen at temperatures of -112 °F (-80 °C) at institutions worldwide that were part of the Frozen Ark Consortium. When stored properly, cells, upon thawing, are viable and able to reproduce. They potentially could be used to resurrect species that have gone extinct and to augment populations of currently endangered species. Thus, the genetic material preserved as part of the Frozen Ark project was of practical value to conservation and breeding programs.

By 2012, the Frozen Ark held 48,000 samples, representing more than 5,500 species of animals. Zoos and aquariums had played a critical role in supplying samples for storage.

used to resurrect extinct species. For example, cells collected from a frozen woolly mammoth could be used as nuclear donors for enucleated elephant eggs. Proof of principle for such "resurrection" was provided by an experiment in which mice were cloned using somatic cell nuclei derived from a mouse that was frozen for more than fifthteen years.

## GENETICALLY MODIFIED ORGANISMS

Reproductive cloning technology has played a key part in the production of genetically modified organisms (GMOs). GMOs are organisms whose genomes have been engineered in the laboratory in order to favour the expression of desired physiological traits or the production of desired biological products. In conventional livestock production, crop farming, and even pet breeding, it has long been the practice to breed select individuals of a species in order to produce offspring that have desirable traits. In genetic modification, however, recombinant genetic technologies are employed to produce organisms whose genomes have been precisely altered at the molecular level, usually by the inclusion of genes from unrelated species of organisms that code for traits that would not be obtained easily through conventional selective breeding.

GMOs are produced using scientific methods that include recombinant DNA technology and reproductive cloning. Reproductive cloning technology generates offspring that are genetically identical to the parent, Dolly being the first animal produced using SCNT technology. Clones of pigs, horses, dogs, and other animals have since been generated using SCNT. Recombinant DNA technology, on the other hand, involves the insertion of one or more individual genes from an organism of one species into the DNA of another. Whole-genome replacement, involving the transplantation of one bacterial genome into the cell body, or cytoplasm, of another microorganism, has been reported, although the technology is still limited to basic scientific applications.

GMOs produced through genetic technologies have become a part of everyday life, entering into society through agriculture, medicine, research, and environmental management. However, while GMOs have benefited human society in many ways, some disadvantages exist. Therefore, the production of GMOs remains a highly controversial topic in many parts of the world.

## GMOS IN AGRICULTURE

Genetically modified (GM) crops have changed the landscape of agriculture. Though GM crops were studied in field trials beginning in the 1980s, the first GM crop to receive approval for commercial production was a type of engineered tobacco, approved

for commercialization in the early 1990s in China for seed production. The first GM plant commercialized as food was a type of tomato, approved in the United States in 1994. Land devoted to the production of GM crops has since expanded dramatically. By late 2010, GM crops were planted across one-tenth of the world's farmland.

GM crops can be used to meet a variety of agricultural needs. For example, the use of wide-spectrum insecticides dropped in areas where plants modified through the addition of a gene from the bacterium *Bacillus thuringiensis* were grown. The bacterium synthesizes a natural insecticide known as Bt toxin. Studies of Bt cotton grown in India found increased yields ranging from 30 to 80 percent. The improved yields were thought to be due to the GM cotton's ability to overcome bollworm infestation. In the United States, Bt cotton was found to have only small gains in yield. In China, Bt cotton initially was successful, but after about four years, populations of insect pests other than bollworm increased, necessitating the use of broad-spectrum pesticides and thereby eliminating the benefits of reduced pesticide spraying with Bt cotton.

GM plants have also been engineered to be resistant to certain chemical herbicides. Such

*A plant biotechnologist inspects a GM "golden rice" plant in the Philippines. Golden rice is a variety of rice to which the gene for beta-carotene (a precursor of vitamin A) has been added. It was developed for use in places where rice is a dietary staple and vitamin-A deficiency is widespread. Besides modifying plants to augment the production of certain nutrients, scientists can also engineer plants to increase crop yields, to help reduce the need for chemical insecticides, and to endure certain weather extremes.*

herbicide-resistant crops (HRC) allow farmers to spray herbicides to control weeds, without causing harm to the crop plants. HRCs, however, are controversial, since they encourage rather than discourage chemical application to the soil.

## GMOS IN MEDICINE AND RESEARCH

GMOs have emerged as one of the mainstays of biomedical research since the 1980s. For example, GM animal models of human genetic diseases enabled researchers to test novel therapies and to explore the roles of candidate risk factors and modifiers of disease outcome. GM microbes, plants, and animals also revolutionized the production of complex pharmaceuticals by enabling the generation of safer and cheaper vaccines and therapeutics. Pharmaceutical products range from recombinant hepatitis B vaccine produced by GM baker's yeast to injectable insulin (for diabetics) produced in GM *Escherichia coli* bacteria and to factor VIII (for hemophiliacs) and tissue plasminogen activator (tPA, for heart attack or stroke patients), both of which are produced in GM mammalian cells grown in laboratory culture. Furthermore, GM plants that produce "edible vaccines" are under development. Such plants, which are engineered to express antigens derived from microbes or parasites that infect the digestive tract, might someday offer a safe, cheap, and painless way to provide vaccines worldwide, without concern for the availability of refrigeration or sterile needles. Novel DNA vaccines may be useful in the struggle to prevent diseases that have proved resistant to traditional vaccination approaches, including HIV/AIDS, tuberculosis, and cancer.

The genetic modification of insects has become an important area of research, especially in the struggle to prevent parasitic diseases. For example, GM mosquitoes have been developed that express a small protein called SM1, which blocks entry of the malaria parasite, *Plasmodium*, into the mosquito's gut. The process results in the disruption of the parasite's life cycle and renders the mosquito malaria-resistant. Introduction of the GM mosquitoes into the wild may someday help eradicate transmission of the malaria parasite without widespread use of harmful chemicals such as DDT or disruption of the normal food chain.

Finally, genetic modification of humans, or so-called gene therapy, is becoming a treatment option for diseases ranging from rare metabolic disorders to cancer. Coupling stem cell technology with recombinant DNA methods may someday allow stem cells derived from a patient to be modified in the laboratory to introduce a desired gene. For example, a normal beta-globin gene may be introduced into the DNA of bone marrow-derived hematopoietic stem cells from a patient with sickle cell anemia, and introduction of these GM cells into the patient could cure the disease without the need for a matched donor.

# PHARMING

Pharming is the generation of pharmaceuticals using animals or plants that have been genetically engineered. Pharming is a useful alternative to traditional pharmaceutical development because genetically engineered livestock and plants are relatively inexpensive to produce and maintain. In addition, a small number of pharmed animals or a small field or greenhouse of pharmed plants can generate large quantities of pharmaceuticals, such as hormones, antibodies, enzymes, and vaccines. However, despite those advantages, pharming remains controversial due to concerns about the safety of pharmed agents and their production.

One of the first mammals engineered successfully for the purpose of pharming was a sheep named Tracy, born in 1990 and created by scientists led by Ian Wilmut at Roslin Institute in Scotland. Tracy was created from a zygote that had been genetically engineered through DNA injection to produce milk containing large quantities of the human enzyme alpha-1 antitrypsin, a substance used to treat cystic fibrosis and emphysema. In 1997 Wilmut and his colleagues generated another pharmed sheep named Polly, a Poll Dorset clone made from nuclear transfer using a fetal fibroblast nucleus genetically engineered to express a human gene known as FIX. The gene encodes a substance called human factor IX, a clotting factor that occurs naturally in most people but that is absent in people with hemophilia, who require replacement therapy with a therapeutic form of the substance. Polly, along with two other sheep engineered to produce human factor IX that also were born in 1997, represented a major advance in animal pharming.

The first pharmed agent produced by animals to gain approval for therapeutic use was recombinant human antithrombin (marketed as ATrynQR), an agent that inhibits blood clotting and that is used for the prevention of heart attack and stroke in high-risk patients. The agent is secreted in the milk of genetically engineered goats. It is then isolated and purified from the milk, which is subject to rigorous safety testing, including analysis for the presence of pathogens (disease-causing organisms).

A variety of plants, including corn, rice, potatoes, tomatoes, tobacco, and alfalfa, have been investigated for their pharming potential. Plant-made pharmaceuticals (PMPs) differ from naturally occurring therapeutic plant compounds because pharmed plants are genetically engineered to express a gene that produces a therapeutic substance. That factor also distinguishes pharmed plants from plants genetically modified for agricultural purposes. PMPs can be extracted and purified from seeds, leaves, or tubers, depending on the type of plant. An example of an agent that has been investigated for rapid production in plants is a vaccine against H5N1, the virus that causes avian influenza (bird flu). The production of the vaccine has been tested in several different plants, including alfalfa and tobacco. However, the need for regulations to prevent the introduction of PMPs into the environment and the food supply has proved to be a significant obstacle to the advancement of plant pharming.

## ROLE OF GMOS IN ENVIRONMENTAL MANAGEMENT

Another application of GMOs is in the management of environmental issues. For example, some bacteria can produce biodegradable plastics, and the transfer of that ability to microbes that can be easily grown in the laboratory may enable the wide-scale "greening" of the plastics industry. Zeneca, a British company, developed a microbially produced biodegradable plastic called Biopol. The plastic was made using a GM bacterium, *Ralstonia eutropha*, to convert glucose and a variety of organic acids into a flexible polymer. GMOs endowed with the bacterially encoded ability to metabolize oil and heavy metals may provide efficient bioremediation strategies.

Genetic modification technologies may help save endangered species such as the giant panda, whose genome was sequenced in an international effort led by the Beijing Genomics Institute at Shenzhen. Genetic studies of the panda genome may provide insight into why pandas have such low rates of reproductive success in captivity. A likely set of genes to consider for future genetic modification, should the goals of panda conservation warrant it, is the major histocompatibility complex (*MHC*). The *MHC* genes play an important role in regulating immune function and also influence behaviours and physiological patterns associated with reproduction.

## DE-EXTINCTION

De-extinction, or resurrection biology, is the process of resurrecting species that have died out, or gone extinct. Although once considered a fanciful notion, the possibility of bringing extinct species back to life has been raised by advances in selective breeding, genetics, and reproductive cloning technologies. Key among those advances was the development of SCNT.

In 2009, using SCNT, scientists very nearly achieved de-extinction for the first time, attempting to bring back the extinct Pyrenean ibex (or bucardo, *Capra pyrenaica pyrenaica*). A clone was produced from preserved tissues, but it died from a severe lung defect within minutes of being born. The near success of the attempt sparked debate about whether species should be brought back from extinction and, if they are brought back, how it should be done and how the species should be managed. The candidate species for de-extinction are many. Some high-profile examples include the woolly mammoth (*Mammuthus primigenius*), the passenger pigeon (*Ectopistes migratorius*), the thylacine (*Thylacinus cynocephalus*), and the gastric-brooding frog (*Rheobatrachus silus*). De-extinction does not extend to dinosaurs, partly because of the extreme old age of specimens and the severe degradation of DNA over time.

The possibility of bringing extinct species back to life was first explored in the early 20th century, through an approach known as back breeding (or breeding back). Back breeding, for the production of a breed that displays the traits of a wild ancestor, is based on the principles of selective breeding, which humans have used for centuries to develop animals with desired traits. In the 1920s and '30s, German zoologists Lutz and Heinz Heck crossbred different types of cattle in an attempt to back breed for an animal that resembled the aurochs (*Bos primigenius*), an extinct species of European wild ox ancestral to modern cattle. The Heck brothers crossbred modern cattle based on historical descriptions and bone specimens that provided morphological information about the aurochs but had no insight into the animals' genetic relatedness. As a consequence, the resulting Heck cattle bore little resemblance to the aurochs.

In the latter part of the 20th century, tools emerged that enabled scientists to isolate and analyze DNA from the bones, hair, and other tissues of dead animals. Coupled with advances in reproductive technologies such as in vitro fertilization (IVF), researchers were able to identify cattle that are close genetic relatives of the aurochs and combine their sperm and eggs to produce an animal (the so-called tauros) that is morphologically and genetically similar to the aurochs.

Other advances in genetic technologies have raised the possibility of inferring and reconstructing the genetic sequences of extinct species from even poorly preserved or cryopreserved specimens. Reconstructed

*An aurochs is an extinct wild ox of Europe in the family Bovidae, from which cattle are probably descended. The possibility of bringing extinct species back to life has been raised by advances in cloning technologies and by developments in in vitro fertilization and in the extraction of DNA from bones, hair, and other tissues of dead and fossilized animals.*

sequences could be compared against the sequences of extant species, allowing for the identification of not only living species or breeds best suited for back breeding but also genes that would be candidates for editing in living species. Genome editing, a technique of synthetic biology, involves adding or removing specific pieces of DNA in a species's genome. The discovery of CRISPR (clustered regularly interspaced short palindromic repeats), a naturally occurring enzyme system that edits DNA in certain microorganisms, greatly facilitated the refinement of genome editing for de-extinction.

Cloning for de-extinction has centred primarily on the use of SCNT. In SCNT carried out for de-extinction, the idea is to transplant the reconstructed embryo into the uterus of a female from a species closely related to the one that is being cloned. In the attempt to resurrect the extinct Pyrenean ibex in 2009, researchers transferred nuclei from thawed fibroblasts of cryopreserved skin specimens into enucleated eggs of domestic goats. The reconstructed embryos were transplanted into either Spanish ibex or hybrid (Spanish ibex x domestic goat) females.

It may also be possible to use stem cells to resurrect extinct species. Somatic cells can be reprogrammed through the introduction of specific genes, creating induced pluripotent stem cells. Such cells can be stimulated to differentiate into different cell types, including sperm and eggs that potentially can give rise to living organisms. Similar to the other techniques of de-extinction, however, the success of an approach based on stem cells depends largely on the quality of DNA that is available in preserved specimens.

## THE COMMERCIALIZATION OF GMOS

In the United States, prior to the issuance in 2009 of guidelines to oversee the development and

*These zebrafish, known as GloFish, originally were genetically engineered to glow in order to assist scientists in studying pollution. They are the only example of genetically engineered animals that are sold commercially to the general public in the United States (as a pet, not as food).*

commercialization of genetically engineered animals, the only such animals that were sold commercially were those used in laboratory research. (A glow-in-the-dark zebrafish, known as GloFish, was the only exception.) After 2009, under the Food and Drug Administration (FDA) new animal drug provisions, genetically engineered animals or products derived from them were prohibited from being sold until the FDA had reviewed and approved them. From that time on, food products from clones of animal species traditionally used for food were considered to be suitable for entry into the U.S. food and animal feed supply. Those products joined the small handful of products derived from genetically engineered bacteria that had already been approved for sale in the United States. Recombinant bovine somatotropin (rBST), for example, was approved by the FDA in 1993 to augment milk production in lactating cows. Insulin produced from genetically modified bacteria was another example of an already approved GMO product.

Many other countries have similar or more stringent barriers to the commercialization of GMOs and products derived from them. The European Union (EU) has notably strict regulations. For example, rBST was removed from the market in European countries in 2000, citing public health safety concerns. The agriculture committee of the European Parliament requested a ban in European countries on the cloning of food animals and food derived from cloned animals. The EU ultimately settled on the requirement for authorization as a means of regulating food from cloned animals, which is considered "novel food."

The reasons for the complex regulatory barriers guiding the use of GMOs and products from them were primarily scientific and social in origin. Public perspectives on the prospect of consuming food products originating from cloned livestock, for example, varied widely. In some parts of the world, the consumption of clone-derived food products met with public skepticism. In general, although studies had suggested that such products were safe to consume, more research was needed, and little was known about the long-term safety of their consumption.

The commercialization of genetically engineered plants has been more successful. The first commercialized, genetically engineered seeds were introduced in the 1990s in the United States. Since then, genetically engineered seeds, particularly for cotton, corn, and soybean, have been adopted by many farmers across the country. Most genetically engineered crops planted on U.S. farmland possess traits for insect resistance or herbicide tolerance. Likewise, in Europe and other countries worldwide, a variety of genetically modified crop plants have been authorized for commercialization.

CHAPTER FIVE

# THERAPEUTIC CLONING

The ability to derive embryonic stem cells (ESCs) from embryos produced through SCNT has given cloning technology special significance in the area of medicine. Known as therapeutic cloning, the application of cloning in medicine is limited to the use of cloned embryos for the purpose of extracting stem cells from them, without ever implanting the embryos in a womb.

The power of therapeutic cloning lies in its ability to allow for the cultivation of stem cells that are genetically identical to a patient. The stem cells could be stimulated to differentiate into any of the more than 200 cell types in the human body. The differentiated cells then could be transplanted into the patient to replace diseased or damaged cells with a lowered risk of rejection by the immune system. The cells could be used to treat a variety of conditions, including Alzheimer disease, Parkinson disease, diabetes mellitus, stroke, and spinal cord injury. In addition, stem cells could be used for in vitro (laboratory) studies of normal and abnormal embryo development or for testing drugs to see if they are toxic or cause birth defects.

## STEM CELLS FROM HUMAN EMBRYOS

Although stem cells have been derived from the cloned embryos of animals such as mice, the generation of stem cells from cloned primate embryos has proven exceptionally difficult. For example, in 2007 stem cells successfully derived from cloned macaque embryos were able to differentiate into mature heart cells and brain neurons. However, the experiment started with 304 egg cells and resulted in the development of only two lines of stem cells, one of which had an abnormal Y chromosome. Likewise, the production of stem cells from human embryos has been fraught with the challenge of maintaining embryo viability. In 2001 scientists at Advanced Cell Technology, a research company in Massachusetts, successfully transferred DNA from human cumulus cells, which are cells that cling to and nourish human eggs, into eight enucleated eggs. Of the eight eggs, three developed into early-stage embryos (containing four to six cells). However, the embryos survived only long enough to divide once or twice.

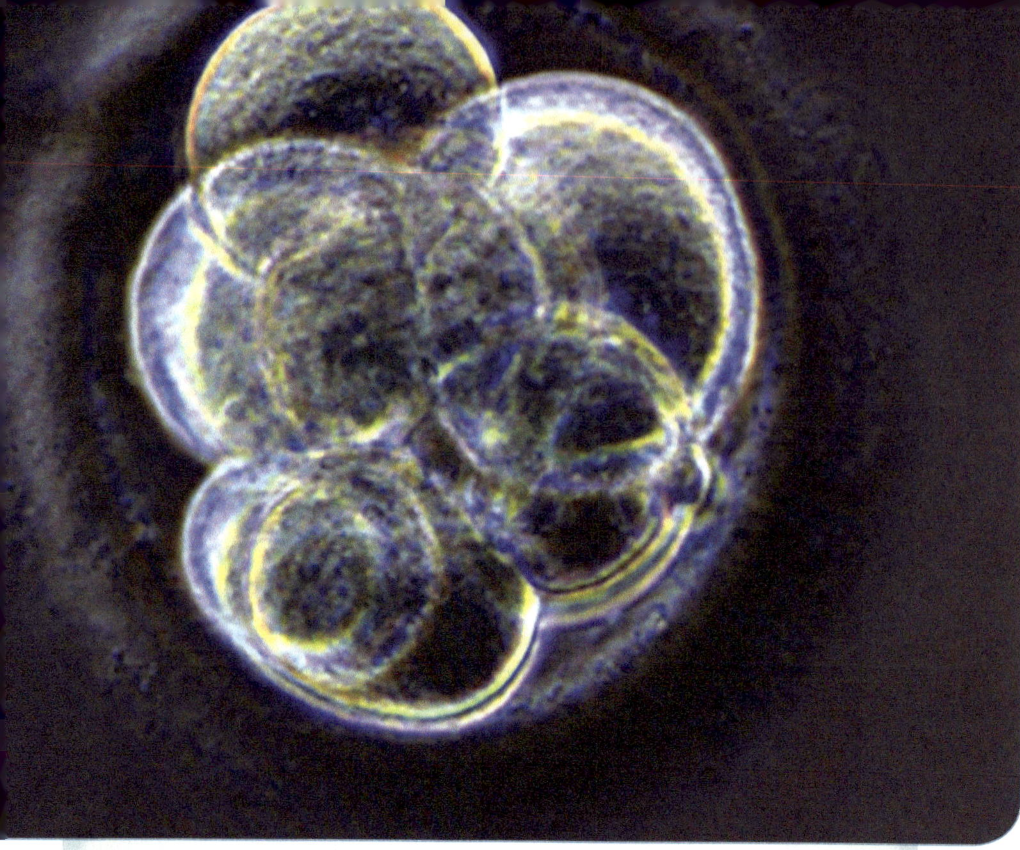

*A cloned human embryo, created by the Centre for Life in Newcastle upon Tyne, England, is seen here three days after the nuclear transfer was completed in 2005. The research team at the centre created a blastocyst by inserting DNA from embryonic stem cells into an unfertilized human egg and inducing it to multiply.*

In 2004 South Korean researcher Hwang Woo-Suk claimed to have cloned human embryos using SCNT and to have extracted stem cells from the embryos. However, that claim later proved to be a fraud. Hwang had fabricated evidence and had actually carried out the process of parthenogenesis, in which an unfertilized egg begins to divide with only half a genome. The following year a team of researchers from the University of

Newcastle upon Tyne was able to grow a cloned human embryo to the 100-cell blastocyst stage using DNA from embryonic stem cells, though they did not generate a line of stem cells from the blastocyst. Scientists have since successfully derived embryonic stem cells from human embryos produced with SCNT.

Progress in research on therapeutic cloning in humans has been slow relative to the advances made in reproductive cloning in animals. That is primarily because of the technical challenges and ethical controversy arising from the procuring of human eggs solely for research purposes. In addition, the development of induced pluripotent stem cells, which are derived from somatic cells that have been reprogrammed to an embryonic state through the introduction of specific genetic factors into the cell nuclei, has challenged the use of cloning methods and of human eggs.

## REGENERATIVE MEDICINE AND STEM CELLS

Advances in biotechnology and stem cell research have tremendous potential particularly in the field of regenerative medicine. Regenerative medicine centres on the application of treatments developed to replace tissues damaged by injury or disease. The treatments may involve the use of biochemical techniques to induce tissue regeneration directly at the site of damage or the use of transplantation

## HWANG WOO-SUK

South Korean scientist Hwang Woo-Suk, who was born on December 15, 1953, in Buyeo, South Korea, debuted the first cloned dog, Snuppy, an Afghan hound, in 2005. That success was later overshadowed by his revolutionary claims of having cloned human embryos from which he extracted stem cells—claims that were discredited as fabricated.

Hwang studied at the College of Veterinary Medicine at Seoul National University, receiving a bachelor's degree (1977) in veterinary medicine and a master's degree (1979) and a doctorate (1982) in theriogenology, the study of animal reproduction. In 1984 he joined the faculty of Hokkaido University in Sapporo, Japan, as a visiting fellow, and from 1986 to 2006 he was a faculty member at Seoul National University.

Hwang earned a name for himself by developing methods for cloning cows and pigs. In 2002, having decided to begin work on human cloning, he partnered with Moon Shin-Yong, an obstetrician who had done extensive work with in vitro fertilization (IVF). In February 2004 Hwang and Moon announced that they had successfully cloned human embryos. They further claimed that one of the embryos had yielded stem cells—undifferentiated cells capable of developing into specific cell types that were believed to have possible applications in treating certain diseases, such as juvenile diabetes, Parkinson disease, and Alzheimer disease. Though Hwang and Moon voiced strong opposition to reproductive cloning and insisted that their research was conducted solely for therapeutic purposes, the announcement heightened public debate regarding bioethics.

Human cells had been cloned before, but the resulting fragile embryos died quickly. Hwang and Moon claimed that the success of their research was due to several factors, including the large number of eggs available to them and the extraction of material from the eggs using a squeezing technique, which supposedly helped to reduce damage.

Hwang published a paper in May 2005 purporting that his team had created 11 individual stem cell lines from cloned embryos. The discovery had significant implications for medicine, as it raised the possibility of treatments tailored to the individual patient, using the patient's own stem cells. In August of that year he also premiered the first cloned dog.

However, in November 2005 Hwang admitted to using eggs donated by two of his own researchers–a practice that violated the principles of scientific ethics. Though Hwang maintained that the researchers had donated the eggs of their own volition, implications of coercion forced him to step down from his position as director of the World Stem Cell Hub, an organization devoted to exploring applications of stem cell technology in medicine. Despite this embarrassment, South Korean public support for him ran high, with hundreds of women volunteering to donate their eggs.

In December of that year, Roh Sung-Il, a colleague on Hwang's project, came forward with information indicating that his human cloning discoveries had been fabricated. An academic review panel at Seoul National University concluded that Hwang, though he had at one point received falsified data from a junior member of his team, had himself been responsible for most of the unfounded assertions made public.

*(continued on the next page)*

*(continued from the previous page)*

The review determined that the only verifiable research that Hwang had conducted in the period of 2004–05 was that which resulted in the cloned dog. Skepticism in the wake of the scandal led to two independent reviews of the dog cloning project, but both ultimately concluded that the research was legitimate.

Hwang was fired from Seoul National University in March 2006, while six members of his team, including Moon, received varying levels of suspension. In 2009, following a three-year trial during which his privileged government-supported lifestyle was made public, Hwang was found guilty of embezzling research funds and illegally purchasing human eggs, for which he received a two-year suspended jail sentence. Hwang then briefly partnered with an American biotechnology firm that specialized in cloning dead pets. Following his evacuation from Libya in February 2011 amid increasing violence there, it emerged that he was in talks with the Libyan government about building a stem cell research centre near Tripoli. He announced in October 2011 that he and his colleagues at the South Korean Sooam Bioengineering Research Institute had cloned coyotes.

techniques employing differentiated cells or stem cells, either alone or as part of a bioartificial tissue.

Bioartificial tissues are made by seeding cells onto natural or biomimetic scaffolds. Natural scaffolds are the total extracellular matrixes (ECMs) of decellularized tissues or organs. In contrast, biomimetic scaffolds may be composed of natural materials, such as collagen or proteoglycans (proteins with long chains of carbohydrate), or built from artificial materials, such as metals, ceramics, or polyester polymers. Cells used for transplants and bioartificial tissues are almost always autogeneic (self) to avoid rejection by the patient's immune system. The use of allogeneic (non-self) cells carries a high risk of immune rejection and therefore requires tissue matching between donor and recipient and involves the administration of immunosuppressive drugs.

## CELL AND BIOARTIFICIAL TISSUE TRANSPLANTATION

A variety of autogeneic and allogeneic cell and bioartificial tissue transplantations have been performed. Examples of autogeneic transplants using differentiated cells include blood transfusion with frozen stores of the patient's own blood and repair of the articular cartilage of the knee with the patients own articular chondrocytes (cartilage cells) that have been expanded in vitro (amplified in number using cell culture techniques in a laboratory). An example of a tissue that has been generated for autogeneic transplant is the human mandible (lower jaw). Functional bioartificial mandibles are made by seeding autogeneic bone marrow cells onto a titanium mesh scaffold loaded with bovine bone matrix, a type of extracellular matrix that has proved valuable in regenerative medicine for its

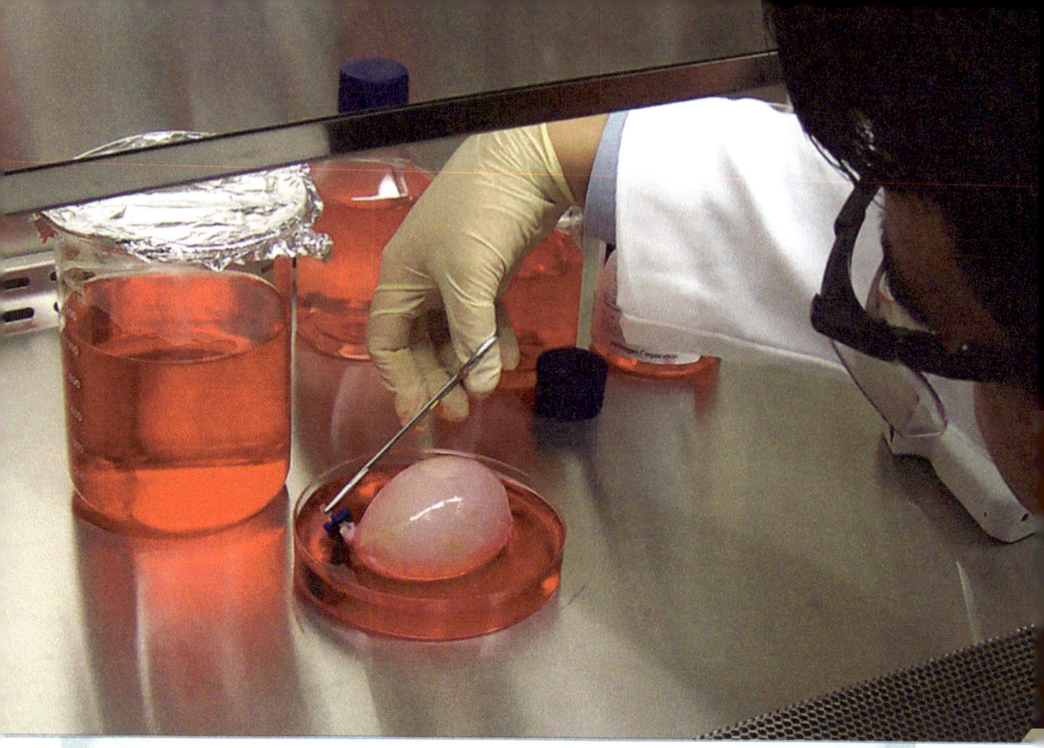

*A doctor at the Institute for Regenerative Medicine at Wake Forest University School of Medicine dips a specially constructed biodegradable mold, or scaffold, which is shaped like a bladder and seeded with human bladder cells, into a growth solution. Bioartificial bladders are used to replace diseased bladders. Because the bioartificial organ is grown from a patient's own tissues, the risk of rejection after it is implanted is reduced.*

ability to promote cell adhesion and proliferation in transplantable bone tissues. Functional bioartificial bladders also have been successfully implanted into patients. Bioartificial bladders are made by seeding a biodegradable polyester scaffold with autogeneic urinary epithelial cells and smooth muscle cells.

Another example of a tissue used successfully in an autogeneic transplant is a bioartificial bronchus, which was generated to replace damaged tissue in a patient affected by tuberculosis. The bioartificial bronchus was constructed from an ECM scaffold of a section of bronchial tissue taken from a donor cadaver. Differentiated epithelial cells isolated from the patient and chondrocytes derived from mesenchymal stem cells collected from the patient's bone marrow were seeded onto the scaffold.

There are few clinical examples of allogeneic cell and bioartificial tissue transplants. The two most common allogeneic transplants are blood-group-matched blood transfusion and bone marrow transplant. Allogeneic bone marrow transplants are often performed following high-dose chemotherapy, which is used to destroy all the cells in the hematopoietic system in order to ensure that all cancer-causing cells are killed. (The hematopoietic system is contained within the bone marrow and is responsible for generating all the cells of the blood and immune system.) That type of bone marrow transplant is associated with a high risk of graft-versus-host disease, in which the donor marrow cells attack the recipient's tissues. Another type of allogeneic transplant involves the islets of Langerhans, which contain the insulin-producing cells of the body. Islets of Langerhans can be transplanted from cadavers to patients with diabetes mellitus, but recipients require immunosuppression therapy to survive. Cell transplant experiments with paralyzed mice, pigs, and nonhuman primates demonstrated that Schwann cells (the myelin-producing cells that insulate nerve axons) injected into acutely injured spinal cord tissue could restore about 70 percent of the tissue's functional capacity, thereby partially reversing paralysis.

## REGENERATION USING STEM CELLS

Studies on experimental animals are aimed at understanding ways in which autogeneic or allogeneic adult stem cells can be used to regenerate damaged cardiovascular, neural, and musculoskeletal tissues in humans. Among adult stem cells that have shown promise in this area are satellite cells, which occur in skeletal muscle fibres in animals and humans. When injected into mice affected by dystrophy, a condition characterized by the progressive degeneration of muscle tissue, satellite cells stimulate the regeneration of normal muscle fibres. Ulcerative colitis in mice was treated successfully with intestinal organoids (organ-like tissues) derived from adult stem cells of the large intestine. When introduced into the colon, the organoids attached to damaged tissue and generated a normal-appearing intestinal lining.

In many cases, however, adult stem cells such as satellite cells have not been easily harvested from their native tissues, and they have been difficult to culture in the laboratory. In contrast, ESCs can be harvested once and cultured indefinitely. Moreover, ESCs are pluripotent, meaning that they can be directed to differentiate into any cell type, which makes them an ideal cell source for regenerative medicine.

Studies of animal ESC derivatives have demonstrated that the cells are capable of regenerating tissues of the central nervous system, heart, skeletal muscle, and pancreas. Derivatives of human ESCs used in animal models have produced similar results. For example, cardiac stem cells from heart-failure patients were engineered to express a protein (Pim-1) that promotes cell survival and proliferation. When the cells were injected into mice that had experienced myocardial infarction (heart attack), the cells were found to enhance the repair of injured heart muscle tissue. Likewise, heart muscle cells (cardiomyocytes) derived from human ESCs improved the function of injured heart muscle tissue in guinea pigs.

Derivatives of human ESCs are likely to produce similar results in humans, although these cells have not been used clinically and could be subject to immune rejection by recipients. The question of immune rejection was by-passed by the discovery in 2007 that adult somatic cells (e.g., skin and liver cells) can be converted to ESCs. The conversion is accomplished by transfecting (infecting) the adult cells with viral vectors carrying genes that encode transcription factor proteins capable of reprogramming the adult cells into pluripotent stem cells. Examples of such factors include *Oct-4*

## JAMES THOMSON

American biologist James Thomson, who was born on December 20, 1958, in Chicago, Illinois, was among the first to isolate human embryonic stem cells and the first to transform human skin cells into stem cells.

Thomson grew up in the Chicago suburb of Oak Park. At the University of Illinois, from which he graduated in 1981 with a bachelor's degree in biophysics, Thomson was encouraged to work in the biology laboratories, where he became interested in the process of early development—the explosive surge of biological activity that occurs when a fertilized egg implants itself in a womb and then begins to divide and form the specialized cells that eventually become the great variety of tissues in the body. He continued his education and research at the University of Pennsylvania, where he gained a doctorate in veterinary medicine in 1985 and a doctorate in molecular biology in 1988. Thomson then completed a postdoctoral fellowship at the Oregon Regional Primate Center (1989–91).

In 1991 Thomson moved to the University of Wisconsin, where he continued his research at the Wisconsin Regional Primate Centre. Having learned in 1980 that biologists had succeeded in extracting embryonic stem cells from mice, Thomson decided to conduct stem cell research on a species much more similar to humans, the rhesus monkey. After many months of painstaking work, he succeeded in isolating the rhesus monkey embryonic stem cells in 1995. That same year he was appointed chief pathologist of the primate centre. The obvious next step, to Thomson, was to try to extract stem cells from human embryos. However, this confronted him with a moral dilemma, as such an extraction is fatal to the embryo. After consulting with several bioethicists at the university, Thomson decided that continued research was ethical as long as the embryos, created by couples who no longer wanted them in order to have children, would otherwise be destroyed. In 1998 he successfully isolated stem cells from a human embryo, almost simultaneously with researchers at Johns Hopkins University. Thomson was appointed scientific director of the WiCell Research Institute, affiliated with the University of Wisconsin, in 1999.

Thomson had assigned the patent for his discovery, which covered both the method of isolating the cells and the cells themselves, to the Wisconsin Alumni Research Foundation. When U.S. President George W. Bush announced in August 2001 that the federal government would only support research on the 64 existing lines (self-sustaining colonies) of human embryonic stem cells, the National Institutes of Health, the agency responsible for implementing the decision, was forced to negotiate with the foundation in order to gain access to the stem cells. Thomson, though disappointed that the Bush edict restricted the creation of new cell lines, was generally pleased that his research could go forward. By November 2007 his team had transformed human skin cells into stem cells—called induced pluripotent stem (iPS) cells—through the insertion of four genes.

Thomson also became an adjunct professor at the University of California, Santa Barbara, in 2007. He was appointed director of regenerative biology at the Morgridge Institute for Research in Madison, Wisconsin, in 2008.

(octamer 4), *Sox-2* (sex-determining region Y box 2), *Klf-4* (Kruppel-like factor 4), and *Nanog*. Reprogrammed adult cells, known as induced pluripotent stem (iPS) cells, are potential autogeneic sources for cell transplantation and bioartificial tissue construction. Such cells have since been created from the skin cells of patients suffering from amyotrophic lateral sclerosis (ALS) and Alzheimer disease and have been used as human models for the exploration of disease mechanisms and the screening of potential new drugs. In one such model, neurons derived from human iPS cells were shown to promote recovery of stroke-damaged brain tissue in mice and rats, and, in another, cardiomyocytes derived from human iPS cells successfully integrated into damaged heart tissue following their injection into rat hearts. Those successes indicated that iPS cells could serve as a cell source for tissue regeneration or bioartificial tissue construction.

## TISSUE SCAFFOLDS AND SOLUBLE REPAIR FACTORS

Scaffolds and soluble factors, such as proteins and small molecules, have been used to induce tissue repair by undamaged cells at the site of injury. The agents protect resident fibroblasts and adult stem cells and stimulate the migration of the cells into damaged areas, where they proliferate to form new tissue. The ECMs of pig small intestine submucosa, pig and human dermis, and different types of biomimetic scaffolds are used clinically for the repair of hernias, fistulas (abnormal ducts or passageways between organs), and burns.

Advances in computer-aided design and nanoparticle- and nanofibre-based bioprinting, and an increasing ability to mimic microenvironments that promote the self-organization of cells into tissues, have enabled the creation of progressively sophisticated scaffolds and bioartificial tissues. Stem cells seeded into nanofibre scaffolds, for example, have been used to create bioartificial articular cartilage and menisci (the incomplete fibrocartilage disks that stretch across the joint cavities). Researchers also have been able to promote significant regeneration in injured mouse latissmus dorsi muscles by seeding muscle stem cells onto strips of ECM from pig bladders and then mechanically "exercising" the tissue by slow contraction and expansion of the strips. Perhaps most remarkably, however, researchers created a bioartificial jellyfish by seeding rat heart muscle cells into an elastic silicone polymer that had been cut to form eight arms projecting from a central disc. The heart cells contracted and relaxed to effectively replicate the pumping action of jellyfish arms.

Advances have also been made in the regeneration of kidney tissue, which poses exceptional technical challenges because of the intricate nature of the structure of the kidney and the complex functions it

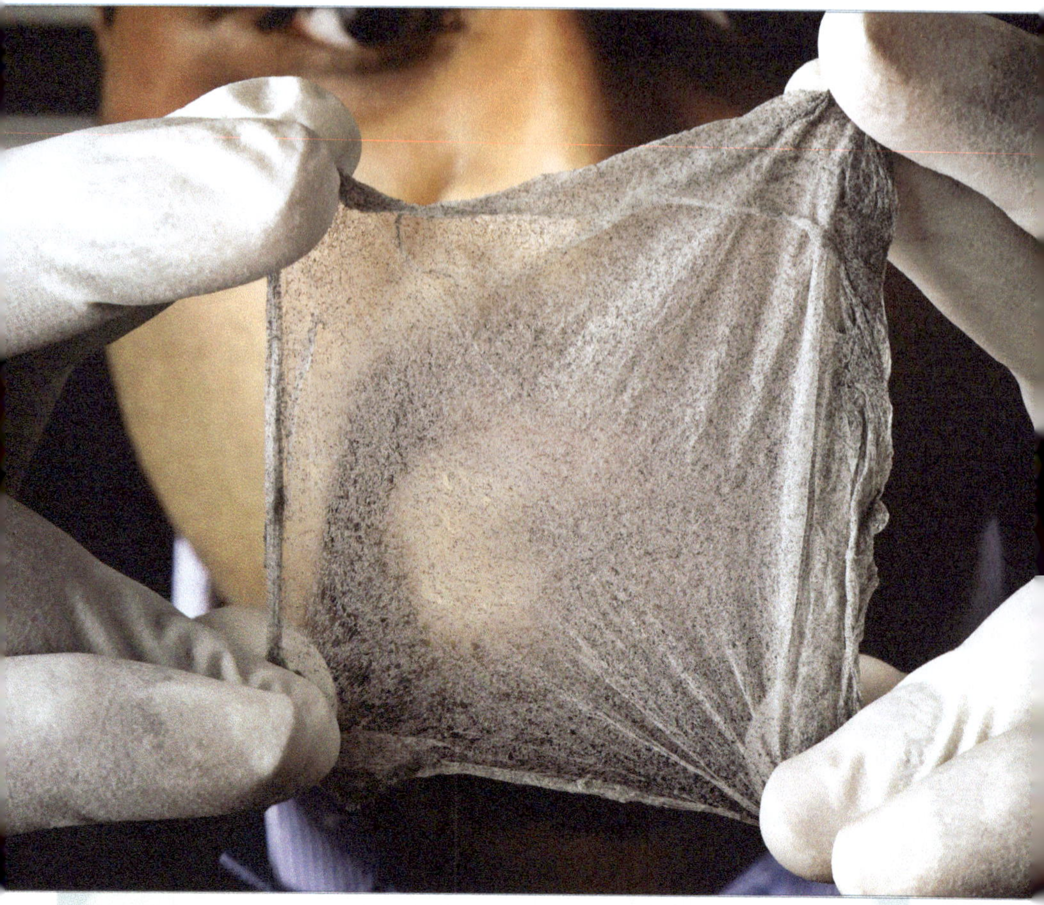

*A researcher holds up a sample of bioartificial tissue that was created by "printing" living cells into a polymer scaffold. In this technique, which is called pressure assisted spinning, three inkjet needles nested inside one another separately deliver living cells, a viscous polymer, and pressurized air. Bioprinters and printers that use a 3D process might someday, many years from now, build artificial tissues and organs for replacement organ surgery.*

performs. In 2013 scientists reported the successful transplantation of bioengineered kidneys into rats. The kidneys were built from decellularized kidney scaffolds that retained the basic organ structure, including the cortical and medullary frameworks, the collecting tubules (which concentrate and transport urine from the nephrons), and the ureters. The bioengineered organs produced urine in rat recipients, retaining about 5 percent of the function of healthy kidneys.

Factors in topical agents—such as platelet-derived growth factor, fibroblast growth factor, and hyaluronate—accelerate the repair of acute and chronic skin wounds and reduce scarring. In animal models of spinal cord injury, factors that inhibit the RhoA pathway, which normally blocks neuronal regeneration, promote axon growth. Growth factors derived from glial cells, a type of non-neuronal cell found in the nervous system, protect neurons that respond to the neurotransmitter dopamine in animal models of Parkinson disease. In addition, a protein called thymosin beta-4 reverses the effects of myocardial infarction in mice.

Screens of synthetic agents aim to find small molecules that suppress scarring, activate resident stem cells, or reprogram somatic cells into stem cells at the site of tissue damage. One such molecule is reversine, which reprograms skin fibroblasts into a stem-cell-like state, enabling them to participate in the regeneration of injured muscle. Further understanding of the molecular biology of wound repair and regeneration will likely result in the design of combinations of scaffolds and soluble natural factors or synthetic small molecules that confer regenerative capacity on regeneration-deficient tissues.

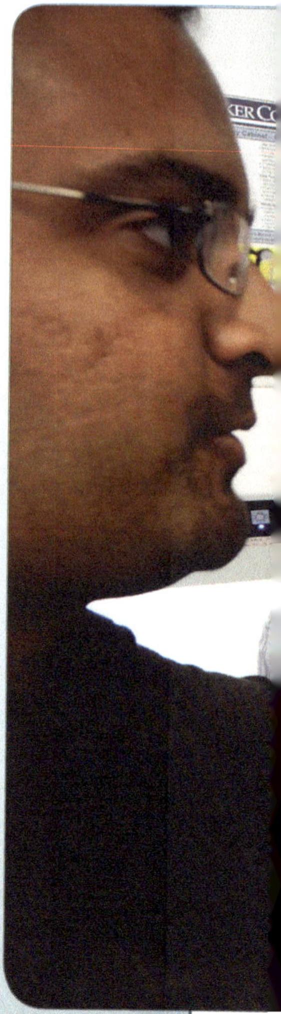

# REPLACING DISEASED TISSUE

Researchers have successfully engineered a variety of biological tissues for the specific purpose of replacing tissues in the human body that have been damaged by injury or disease. The process of developing such biological substitutes forms the basis of tissue engineering.

Tissue engineering emerged in the late 1980s. By the early 1990s the concept of applying engineering to the repair of biological tissue resulted in the rapid growth of tissue engineering as an interdisciplinary field with the potential to revolutionize important areas of medicine.

Tissue engineering integrates biological components, such as cells and growth factors, with engineering principles and synthetic materials. Substitute tissues can be produced by first seeding human cells onto scaffolds, which may be made from collagen or from a biodegradable polymer. The scaffolds are then incubated in mediums containing growth factors, which stimulate the cells to grow and divide. As cells spread across the scaffold, the substitute tissue is formed. This tissue can be implanted into the human body, with the implanted scaffold eventually being either absorbed or dissolved.

Examples of tissues that are candidates for tissue engineering include skin, cartilage, heart, and bone. The production of skin substitutes has played an important role in improving the success

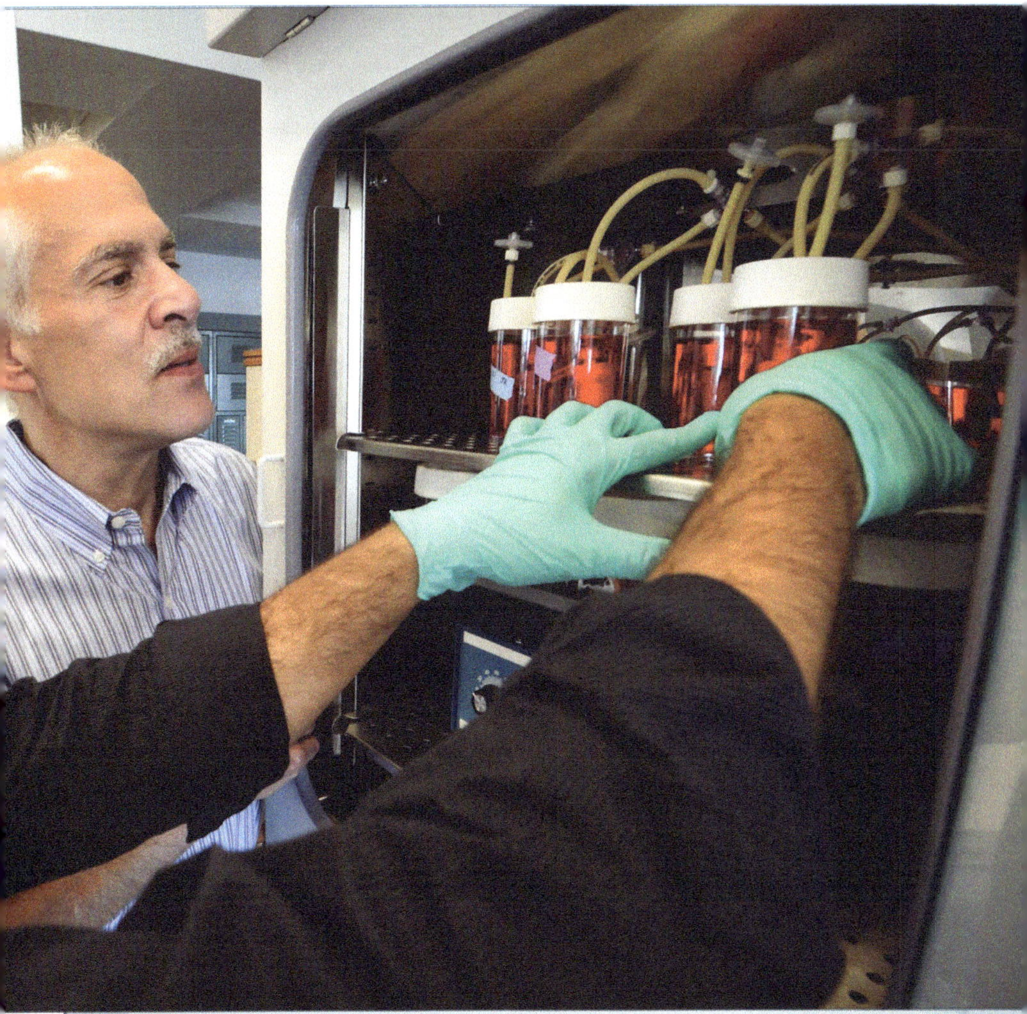

*These scientists at the University of Minneapolis produce tissue-engineered heart valves. The heart valves are grown in a bioreactor.*

of skin graft surgeries, especially for complex wounds such as burns. Substitute tissues of the renal system, including urinary bladders and urethras, have also been engineered and transplanted successfully, thereby broadening therapeutic opportunities for complicated renal disorders.

## THERAPEUTIC CLONING AND GENE THERAPY

Therapeutic cloning also offers promise in the treatment of genetic defects. Combined with gene therapy, therapeutic cloning could allow for the restoration of gene function stemming from loss-of-function mutations. Such mutations reduce or eliminate the activity of specific proteins.

As proof-of-principle, in 2002 researchers reported the successful correction of a genetic defect in mice using a combination of stem cells and gene therapy. Nuclei from adult skin cells in mice affected by a genetic immune deficiency were transferred into enucleated mouse egg cells. ESCs were isolated from the resulting blastocysts, and the genetic mutation was repaired in the ESCs in vitro. Mice with the genetic defect were treated with the repaired ESCs, which partially restored the animals' immune function. In addition, the repair of the genetic mutation in the cloned ESCs had no affect on the cells of the germ line (the cells of the ovary or testis), and thus the repair could not be passed on to the next generation. Germline gene therapy has been a controversial area of research, given its potential to allow for the genetic manipulation of future generations.

In another example, scientists have been pursuing the application of therapeutic cloning and gene therapy to the treatment of Duchenne muscular dystrophy. Duchenne muscular dystrophy is characterized by abnormally low levels or the complete absence of a protein called dystrophin, which plays a role in strengthening and protecting muscle fibres in skeletal and cardiac muscle tissue. The abnormalities in dystrophin arise from genetic mutations. Researchers have been able to correct the abnormal dystrophic phenotype in mice using fibroblast cells

*A biotech researcher in Leiden, the Netherlands, is developing a treatment for Duchenne muscular dystrophy at a laboratory. Such researchers are applying therapeutic cloning and gene therapy to develop RNA-modulating options for the treatment of genetic disorders.*

from the mice that have been reprogrammed into iPS cells. The iPS cells were corrected genetically in vitro, stimulated to differentiate into progenitors of skeletal muscle cells, and then transplanted back into dystrophic mice. The animals experienced improvements in muscle contractile strength. Though more research is needed, successes with cell transplantation and gene therapy in animals has suggested that similar approaches could someday be used in the treatment of humans who suffer from certain types of genetic disease.

CHAPTER SIX

# ETHICAL AND MORAL ISSUES

Since the 1990s, cloning has been, by far, the most controversial issue in bioethics. The cloning of Dolly conjured up in the public imagination alarming visions of armies of identical human clones, and many legislatures hastened to prohibit the reproductive cloning of human beings. But the public's reaction resulted more from ignorance and distaste than reflection, which the popular news media did little to encourage. Some bioethicists suggested that in a free society there are no good reasons—apart from the risk that a cloned human may suffer from genetic abnormalities—for cloning to be prohibited. Others viewed cloning as a violation of human dignity, because it would mean that human beings could be designed by other humans. That objection was forcefully stated by bioethicist Leon Kass, who appealed to what he called, in the title of a 1997 essay, *The Wisdom of Repugnance.*

The culmination of such advances in techniques for influencing human reproduction is the mastery of genetic engineering. By the late 20th century, some couples in the United States paid substantial sums for eggs from women with outstanding test scores at elite colleges. (Payment for eggs or sperm was illegal in most other countries.) In the 21st century, prenatal testing for genetic defects has become common and widespread, especially in older pregnant women. When a defect is discovered, couples may seek the assistance of a genetic counselor, who can help them make informed decisions. In some cases, women may choose to terminate their pregnancy. But in many other instances, information from prenatal testing is used to help expecting parents prepare for the birth of a child affected by a genetic defect.

Owing to advances in techniques used in vitro fertilization (IVF), some genetic tests can be performed on embryos in vitro—before they are implanted into the mother's uterus. As more genetic tests become available, people increasingly will face the question posed by the title of Jonathan Glover's probing book *What Sort of People Should There Be?* (1984). The question addresses one of the most challenging issues for ethics in the 21st century.

## REPRODUCTIVE CLONING OF HUMANS

Human reproductive cloning remains universally condemned, primarily for the psychological, social, and physiological risks associated with cloning. A cloned embryo intended for implantation into a womb requires thorough molecular testing to fully determine whether it is healthy and whether the cloning process is complete. In addition, as demonstrated by 100 failed attempts to generate a cloned macaque in 2007, a viable pregnancy is not guaranteed. Because the risks associated with reproductive cloning in humans introduce a very high likelihood of loss of life, the process is considered unethical.

There are other philosophical issues that also have been raised concerning the nature of reproduction and human identity that reproductive cloning might violate. Concerns about eugenics, the once popular notion that the human species could be improved through the selection of individuals possessing desired traits, also have surfaced, since cloning could be used to breed "better" humans, thus violating principles of human dignity, freedom, and equality.

The decision to clone humans, even for the "betterment" of the species, raises the issues of who would be the ideal candidates for cloning and what characteristics should be duplicated. Among some of the issues debated are whether extreme intelligence or great athleticism, creativity or stability, or health or sensitivity should be more valued. Even thornier are the issues of who would be the people to decide what traits are valuable and which people are chosen to be cloned, if the cloning of humans were to become possible and accepted.

In one sense it would be nearly impossible to produce true duplicates of people. Clones are copies

*A poster that reads "Evolution Is Dead" is displayed at a news conference that is attended by human rights advocates and scientists in 2002. Some attendees urged an international ban on human cloning.*

of genetic information. The process of cloning cannot reproduce the same sequence of experiences in the clone that the original lived through. Most genes provide potential, but experience and environment determine if and to what degree that potential is realized. Identical twins, for example, even those raised in the same household, often have different personalities, interests, attitudes, and other traits. If Albert Einstein were cloned, there would be no guarantee that his clone would excel in math or physics. American basketball player Michael Jordan received extraordinary support from his parents, and so a clone of Jordan, lacking that support, might turn out to be a poor basketball player. Such a clone also could develop a serious illness early in life and be left with poor vision or reflexes. Achieving a specific set of results from a human clone, then, would not be as simple as, say, providing a clone of a prize dairy cow with the nutrition and conditions that would help her achieve her full potential at producing milk. In addition, it must be pointed out that genes can mutate, or suddenly change, as a result of exposure to normal background radiation or certain chemicals or other influences. (Most mutations are lethal, but some are

# THE USES AND ETHICS OF CLONING, BY IAN WILMUT (1997)

The announcement in February 1997 of the birth of Dolly the sheep, the first clone of an adult mammal, attracted international attention because of the new medical and agricultural opportunities and the new ethical concerns raised by the breakthrough. The term *cloning* (derived from the Greek word *klon*, meaning "twig") strictly indicates the taking of a cutting, as in plant breeding, but it has also come to be used to describe the production, by means of a process known as nuclear transfer, of genetically identical animals. Nuclear transfer involves removing the nucleus from an unfertilized egg and replacing it with a nucleus from a donor cell. As it is the transferred nucleus that determines almost all of the characteristics of the resulting offspring, a clone will resemble its "parent," the animal from which the donor cell was taken.

While the most obvious use of cloning is to produce groups of animals that are genetically identical, nuclear transfer also may be used for the introduction of precise genetic changes in mammals. Although other methods have been employed to add genes to mammals, nuclear transfer makes it possible for the first time to change any function of existing genes. Another application of cloning technology is the production of undifferentiated (embryonic) cells, which could be helpful in treating certain diseases. Before there can be significant use of these applications, however, some practical difficulties must be resolved, as only a small proportion of the embryos thus far produced by nuclear transfer have become live offspring.

Ethical choices must also be made. The public response to cloning suggests that countries differ widely in their perceptions of this new technology. Immediately after the announcement of Dolly's birth, for example, Italy banned the cloning of any mammal, whereas a number of groups in the U.S. welcomed the technique.

All of the different tissues of an adult animal or person are derived from the single cell of a fertilized egg. In the early stages of development, the dividing embryonic cells are able to contribute to all of the tissues of the developing embryo before the cells differentiate, progressively, as a result of changes in gene expression. The birth of Dolly by means of an already differentiated adult cell for nuclear transfer showed that the process of differentiation is reversible, at least in some cases. This raises the revolutionary thought that it may be possible to take cells from a human patient and cause them to dedifferentiate to a state in which they are able to contribute to all tissues. If necessary, a genetic change could be made in the cells before they are stimulated to differentiate to the type required for treating a specific disease before return to the patient. Since the cells are identical to the patient, no immune response is expected. This approach has been suggested for the treatment of such varied conditions as AIDS, Duchenne muscular dystrophy, and Parkinson disease.

[In 1997], the only way to induce dedifferentiation [was] to form an embryo from the donor cell and to culture the embryo to the stage when it has a few hundred cells but has not begun to differentiate. As the nervous system would not have begun to develop at that stage, the embryo would have no means of

*(continued on the next page)*

*(continued from the previous page)*

feeling pain or sensing the environment. At this point the cells would be separated and grown in culture. Some people object strongly to this procedure on religious grounds, holding that the embryo has a soul at the moment of conception. As the embryo would have the potential to become a person, they find it deeply disturbing to consider using cells from that embryo for any purpose that would deprive that person of life. An alternative view is that it is justifiable to use the cells since the developing embryo does not become a sentient being until much later in development. Whatever the ethical views, it would be much more practical to develop such cell-based therapies if dedifferentiation could be induced without the production of embryos. Research in 1997 was beginning to assess this possibility. [Editor's note: In 2006 Japanese scientist Shinya Yamanaka succeeded in doing just that. By introducing certain genes into the nucleus of an adult cell, he was able to revert the cell to a pluripotent state. Those cells became known as induced-pluripotent stem (iPS) cells.]

Although the use of cloning to produce copies of humans has been suggested, many people would judge this to be morally wrong. In addition, the prospect of cloning humans raises false expectations, since human personality is only partly determined by genes. Cloning a sick or dying relative would provide a genetically identical copy of that person, but this new individual would likely develop a quite different personality. Similarly, a copy of an athlete, movie star, entrepreneur, or scientist might well choose another career because of chance events during his or her lifetime. One hypothetical scenario involves an infertile couple who wish to make a copy of one or the other partner rather than having a child by artificial insemination. The social concern is that the parents would not be able to treat naturally a child who was a copy of one of them.

The impetus behind the research that led to Dolly was not to find a way to clone humans but rather to develop genetically engineered animals that would serve a variety of purposes. As there are great genetic differences in cattle herds and sheep flocks, breeding copies of selected livestock would increase the efficiency of agricultural productivity and help boost the quality of such commercial products as milk, beef, and wool. As in the management of other breeding schemes, it will be important for scientists to maintain the balance between intense selection of livestock and the maintenance of genetic variability. Preservation of frozen cells from a large number of representatives of different breeds would allow nuclei from those donor cells to be used as required. The ethical issues in animal cloning are perhaps less controversial than with humans. Nevertheless, some people worry that producing large numbers of animal clones only increases the likelihood that these animals will be mistreated.

Genetic modification of livestock will also provide new opportunities in medicine and research. Today many patients in need of transplants die before organs become available from suitable donors. Cloning pigs has been suggested as a means of rapidly achieving xenotransplantation, the use of animal organs to replace organs in human patients. Organs transplanted between species are in danger

*(continued on the next page)*

*(continued from the previous page)*

of being destroyed within minutes by the acute immune response of the body receiving the transplant. However, strategies are being developed to modify pigs genetically so that rejection by the immune system may be effectively prevented.

Another potential medical application of cloning involves cystic fibrosis research. A common hereditary disease of humans caused by errors in a single gene, cystic fibrosis is characterized by difficulty in breathing due to the accumulation of mucus in the lungs. [In 1997] new treatments for cystic fibrosis [were] assessed by being administered either to human patients or to mice bred with the disease. There is, of course, a limit to the risks that may be taken with human patients, and there are significant differences between the respiratory systems of mice and humans. Cloning sheep bred with cystic fibrosis would provide an inexhaustible supply of animals on which to experiment and would overcome the disadvantages of experimenting on humans and mice.

There have been a variety of responses to these proposals. To some people it is ethically unacceptable to alter a species genetically, but those advancing this view must acknowledge that conventional genetic selection has already brought about profound changes in livestock and pet animals. While many people welcome the availability of organs from animals, others are disturbed at the suggestion of deliberately making animals ill, and some would prohibit such a practice whatever the benefit. Provided that a judgment is made that the advance in medical treatment justifies the distress caused to the animal, most societies accept the benefits from studies involving animal experimentation. In most countries legislation permits such research only under strict supervision.

Experience shows that predictions as to the value and uses of new techniques are often wrong and that society changes its assessment of a new procedure over time. Many religious leaders were initially scandalized by the introduction of methods for the artificial insemination of cattle, a procedure that helped eliminate sexually transmitted diseases and provided the single biggest advance in livestock breeding. Great concern was raised at the time of the birth of Louise Brown, the first baby to be produced after in vitro fertilization. Since then thousands of babies have been born to previously infertile couples, and the technique of artificial insemination is widely accepted. It remains to be seen how methods of cloning will be used and how they will be accepted.

—Ian Wilmut, leader of the research team that produced the first clone of an adult mammal at the Roslin Institute, near Edinburgh

not.) Genes occasionally mutate in both clones and nonclones. If a gene mutated early in the embryonic life of a clone, the clone would no longer be a clone because it would not be a duplicate of the ancestor. Some mutations could considerably change the potential of the clone, perhaps even contribute to an untimely death.

If society allows the cloning of people, society and individuals will have to cope with the consequences. For example, some clones of law-abiding, virtuous people could develop into criminals or develop vices the originals never had or were able to control. Also, a seemingly perfect clone might carry a gene that causes a deadly disease early in life under some condition the clone is exposed to but which the ancestor never confronted.

Another issue of concern is the effect that a large population of clones— human or otherwise—would have on an organism's susceptibility to disease and other threats and even on evolution. One advantage to having a wide array of genetic variations within a species is that when a change in the environment arises—such as when a new disease emerges—some individuals may have a gene or genes that allow them to survive the new challenge. Such a gene or genes, though previously not particularly or at all useful and not likely to have been selected for duplication in cloning, might save the species from extinction. Such matters are the basis for much evolution. Swifter and more cunning foxes, for example, catch more rabbits, and therefore are more likely to survive and produce offspring with traits for swiftness and cunning. The fastest rabbits are the most likely to escape and survive and thus the most likely to produce offspring with traits for speed. Thus, the genes that determine all the things that go into improving the speed of those animals are constantly being selected for by nature. If only one rabbit were cloned—even the fastest—and only the rabbit clones existed, sooner or later the foxes, with their greater genetic diversity, would adapt, becoming fast or cunning enough to catch them all.

Without genetic diversity, no species can evolve very well. It may be that even a pure clone population could to some extent adapt to changing conditions. However, it is likely that the speed and the boundaries of such adaptation would be so severely restricted that the rate of environmental change would outpace the clonal population's ability to adapt, forcing its extinction. It appears very likely, then, that there are no species so perfect or so safe, in an evolutionary sense, that their genetic diversity should be eliminated by replacing diverse individuals with clones.

## THE USE OF HUMAN EMBRYOS FOR STEM CELL RESEARCH

As with reproductive cloning, therapeutic cloning also is not without controversy. Of central concern has been the use of human embryos for the generation of ESCs. Some individuals and groups have an objection to the use of human embryos for therapeutic cloning, because the destruction of the embryo is equated with the destruction of a human life, even though that life has not developed past the embryonic stage. Those who are opposed to therapeutic cloning believe that the technique supports and encourages acceptance of the idea that human life can be created and expended for any purpose. However, those who support therapeutic cloning believe that there is a moral imperative to heal the sick and to seek greater scientific knowledge. Many supporters believe that therapeutic and research cloning should be not only allowed but also publicly funded, similar to other types of disease and therapeutics research. Most supporters also argue that the embryo demands special moral consideration, requiring regulation and oversight by funding agencies. In addition, it is important to many philosophers and policy makers that women and couples not be exploited for the purpose of obtaining their embryos or eggs.

There are laws and international conventions that attempt to uphold certain ethical principles and regulations concerning cloning. In 2005 the United Nations passed a nonbinding Declaration on Human Cloning that called upon member states "to adopt all measures necessary to prohibit all forms of human cloning inasmuch as they are incompatible with human dignity and the

*An environmental activist in South Korea protests against a medical team that cloned human cells to create transplant organs. In 2005 the United Nations General Assembly declared an international ban on human cloning, including therapeutic cloning.*

protection of human life." The declaration did not provide leeway for member countries to pursue therapeutic cloning. The United Kingdom, through its Human Fertilisation and Embryology Authority, issues licenses for creating human ESCs through nuclear transfer. The licenses ensure that human embryos are cloned for legitimate therapeutic and research purposes aimed at obtaining scientific knowledge about disease and human development. The licenses require the destruction of embryos by the 14th day of development, since that is when embryos begin to develop the primitive streak, the first indicator of an organism's nervous system.

The regulation of stem cell research in Europe varied by country. In Austria, for example, research on embryos was banned, but research that made use of imported human ESC lines was permitted. In countries such as Bulgaria and Greece, it was legal to use embryos left over from IVF for the derivation of ESCs. Some countries had outright bans on reproductive cloning but allowed research on ESCs. Still other countries had no specific legislation in place that addressed stem cell research or reproductive cloning. In the United States, the federal government has not passed any laws regarding human cloning, due to disagreement about whether to ban all cloning or to ban only reproductive cloning.

In 1995 the Dickey-Wicker amendment was attached to U.S. appropriations bills. It prevented the use of federal dollars to fund the harm or destruction of human embryos for research. It is presumed that nuclear transfer and any other form of cloning is subject to that restriction. The Dickey-Wicker amendment remains the primary legal barrier to performing research on human ESCs in the United States.

In 2001 U.S. President George W. Bush stated that he would allow federal support of research using ESCs, but only on cell lines that already existed and had been derived from leftover embryos grown in infertility clinics. That restriction, according to Bush, would permit research "without crossing a fundamental moral line by providing taxpayer funding that would sanction or encourage further destruction of human embryos that have at least the potential for life." Many research scientists considered the decision severely limiting, and in September of that year, a committee of the Institute of Medicine (IOM), a branch of the U.S. National Research Council, issued a report concluding that new cell lines would still be needed down the road, in part because the existing lines would likely accumulate harmful genetic mutations over time.

In November 2001, a private Massachusetts biotechnology firm, Advanced Cell Technology, provoked fury when it announced that it had taken the first steps toward cloning human embryos. According to the company, the goal was not to clone a human being but to produce stem cells for treating disease. In fact, most of the embryos died before reaching even an eight-cell stage, without producing the desired stem cells. President Bush, religious and political leaders, and many scientists condemned the work as immoral and a dangerous move in the wrong direction.

In 2009, under President Barack Obama, restrictions on federally funded stem cell research were relaxed. With Executive Order 13505, Removing Barriers to Responsible Scientific Research Involving Human Stem Cells, Obama introduced new guidelines on ESC research. The guidelines allowed for federally supported research with human stem cells, including human ESCs, so long as the work was deemed scientifically worthy and within the bounds permitted by law, namely the Dickey-Wicker amendment. Specifically, the guidelines permitted the government to fund research that used ESCs derived from human embryos that had been generated for reproductive purposes with in vitro fertilization but were no longer needed. The embryos could be used only with the informed consent of the donor.

*President Barack Obama congratulates Representative Jim Langevin of Rhode Island, the first quadriplegic to serve in the U.S. House of Representatives, after Obama signed an Executive Order to reverse the federal government's ban on funding stem-cell research in 2009.*

# ETHICAL AND SOCIAL ISSUES: GMOS, DE-EXTINCTION, AND GENE THERAPY

## SOCIOPOLITICAL RELEVANCE OF GMOS

While GMOs offer many potential benefits to society, the potential risks associated with them have fueled controversy, especially in the food industry. Many skeptics warn about the dangers that GM crops may pose to human health. For example, genetic manipulation may potentially alter the allergenic properties of crops. However, the more-established risk involves the potential spread of engineered crop genes to native flora and the possible evolution of insecticide-resistant "superbugs." In 1998 the European Union (EU) addressed such concerns by implementing strict GMO labeling laws and a moratorium on the growth and import of GM crops. In addition, the stance of the EU on GM crops has led to trade disputes with the United States, which, by comparison, has accepted GM foods openly. Other countries, such as Canada, China, Argentina, and Australia, also have open policies on GM foods, but some African states have rejected international food aid containing GM crops.

The use of GMOs in medicine and research has produced a debate that is more philosophical in nature. For example, while researchers in genetics believe they are working to cure disease and ameliorate suffering, many people worry that current genetic approaches to therapy may one day be applied to produce "designer" children or to lengthen the natural human life span. Similar to many other technologies, the production and application of GMOs can be used to address and resolve complicated scientific, medical, and environmental issues, but they must be used wisely.

## ETHICAL CONSIDERATIONS OF DE-EXTINCTION

Cloning, stem cell manipulation, genome reconstruction, and genome editing are powerful technologies with significant ethical ramifications when applied to de-extinction. The expense and inefficiency of SCNT, for example, has raised questions about its practicality for resurrecting extinct species.

Perhaps the greatest concern, however, is the potential of those technologies, as well as back breeding, to alter the course of natural history. De-extinction provides an opportunity for humans to rectify past harms inflicted on other species, as well as to expand species diversity. But many extinct species were driven out of existence as a result of habitat loss, and others lived in habitats that have since been altered dramatically. In addition, in the

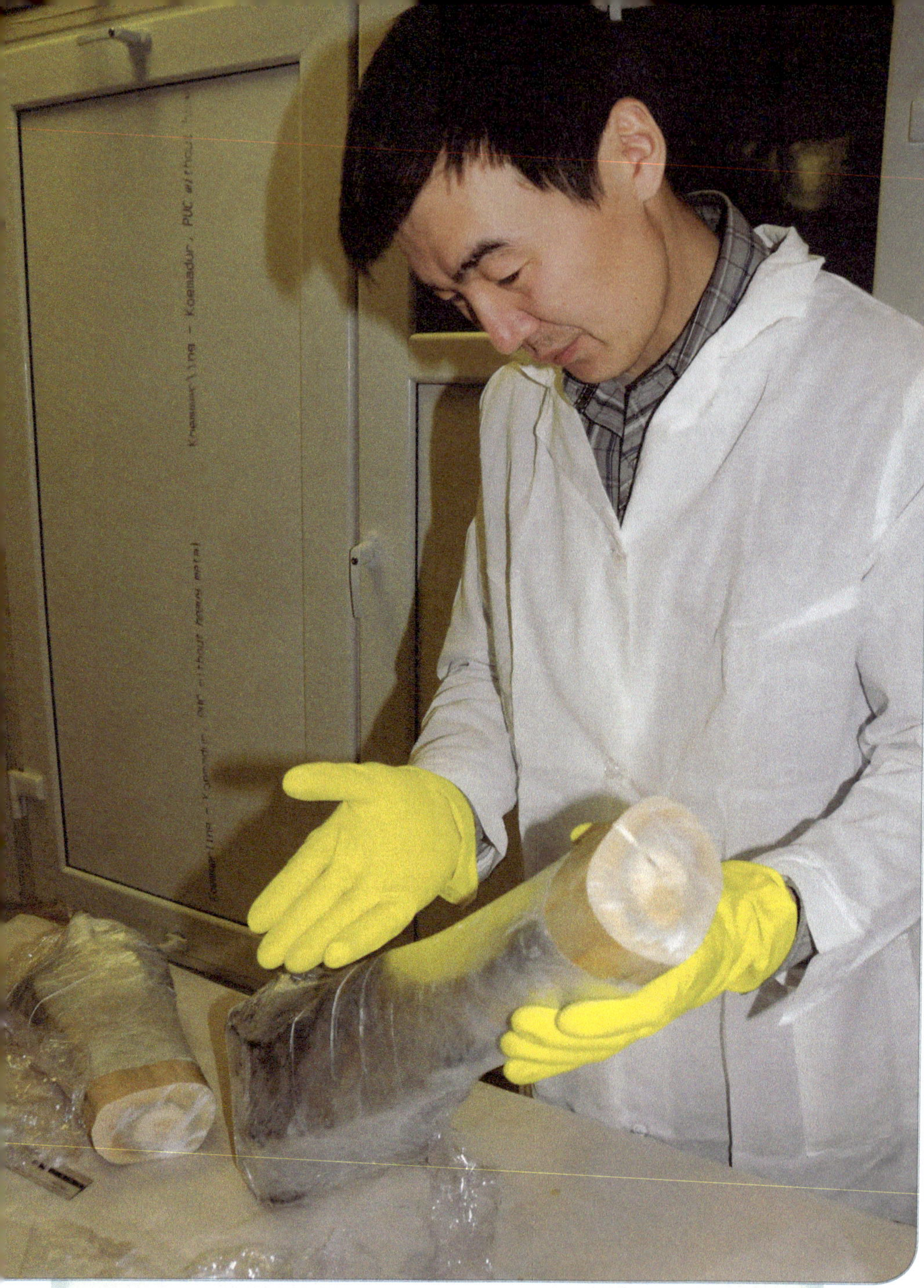

*A scientist displays a cross-section of a mammoth's thighbone at the Sakha Republic's mammoth museum in 2011. Japanese and Russian scientists stated that discovering well-preserved bone marrow in permafrost soil in Siberia might increase the chance of cloning the extinct animal.*

near term, resurrected species would be considered endangered and would therefore require conservation, for which resources often are constrained or lacking. De-extinction, by providing the option to bring species back later, also could have the unintended consequence of condoning extinction and could give impetus to endeavours that threaten biodiversity.

Other concerns include unknowns about the fate of resurrected animals, from the health of cloned individuals to whether the animals would be able to adapt to current environmental conditions and whether they would be able to produce viable offspring. The classification of species revived through back breeding, cloning, or genetic reconstruction, all of which could involve divergence from an extinct species' original genetic constitution, also remains uncertain. The potential to be leveraged as a means of advancing financial and commercial interests has led some to question the motivation of researchers and companies behind certain de-extinction projects.

Nonetheless, de-extinction has helped fuel important progress in science, building particularly on knowledge in developmental biology and genetics. It also has generated interest in endangered species, with many of the tools of de-extinction also being applicable to the conservation of endangered species. The reconstruction of extinct genes could be used, for example, to restore genetic diversity in threatened species or subspecies.

## CONCERNS RELATED TO THERAPEUTIC CLONING FOR GENE THERAPY

Therapeutic cloning for gene therapy has likewise raised ethical concerns, most of which centre around gene therapy as a form of genetic manipulation. The correction of genetic defects is seen by some as a means of redesigning the human genome. Of special concern has been germline gene therapy, which if carried out successfully would allow for the correction of genetic mutations that could be passed on offspring. For those who receive such therapy, the gene corrections most likely would be seen as beneficial. Some people have also raised concerns about the possibility for inadvertent effects on the germline from gene therapy intended for only somatic cells.

# CONCLUSION

Since the early 20th century, when Hans Spemann first twinned salamander embryos, scientists have made amazing progress in cloning. They not only developed the means to apply cloning in research, agriculture, and medicine but also continue to push the boundaries of biology. With advancements in cloning techniques for stem cell research, for example, scientists have been able to explore human diseases at a cellular level, attempting to better understand the cellular mechanisms involved in disease. In doing so, they have begun to create opportunities for the development of new, potentially more-effective treatments for complex conditions, such as Duchenne muscular dystropy, cystic fibrosis, and spinal cord injury.

The ability to induce pluripotentcy in adult cells, producing iPS cells, has enabled scientists to generate cellular models of disease. In 2014, for example, researchers developed a cellular model of Parkinson disease by generating iPS cells from skin cells of an individual diagnosed with the disease. They also created a cell model with iPS cells from the individual's identical twin, who was unaffected by Parkinson disease. After comparing the two models, the researchers found that neurons

*Dr. Jeanne Loring is the principal investigator at The Center for Regenerative Medicine at The Scripps Research Institute in La Jolla, California. The research undertaken at this lab involves pluripotent stem cells and their use in regenerative medicine. Major projects include the development of stem cell therapies for Parkinson disease, multiple sclerosis, and autism.*

grown from the affected twin's cells were deficient in the neurotransmitter dopamine but had elevated levels of an enzyme known as monoamine oxidase B (MAO-B). Using treatments to reduce MAO-B activity and to decrease the levels of an enzyme called glucocerebrosidase, production of which is linked to risk of Parkinson disease, they were able to restore dopamine levels in the Parkinson disease model. The findings suggested that the combination therapy could be effective against the disease. The novel insights would not have been possible without advances in cloning and stem cell technology.

**BIOINFORMATICS** The collection, classification, storage, and analysis of biochemical and biological information using computers, especially as applied in molecular genetics and genomics.

**BLASTOCYST** A distinct stage of an animal embryo. A blastocyst is composed of an inner cell mass and an enveloping layer.

**CLONE** An individual that is genetically identical to another individual.

**DE-EXTINCTION** Resurrection biology; the process of bringing extinct species back to life.

**DIFFERENTIATE** Become specialized.

**DIOECIOUS** Relating to animals in which sperm and eggs are produced by separate sexes.

**EMBRYOLOGIST** A specialist in embryology, a branch of biology that deals with embryos and their development.

**EMBRYONIC STEM CELL (ESC)** A stem cell that is derived from the inner cell mass of a mammalian embryo at a very early stage of development, when it is composed of a hollow sphere or dividing cells.

**ENUCLEATED** Not having a nucleus.

**GAMETE** The basic unit of sexual reproduction.

**GENOME** The genetic material of an organism.

**HAPLOID** Having the number of chromosomes characteristic of germ cells or half the number characteristic of body cells.

**HOMOLOGOUS** Derived from or developed in response to organisms of the same species.

**INDUCED-PLURIPOTENT STEM (IPS) CELL** A reprogrammed adult cell.

**MEIOSIS** The cellular process that results in the number of chromosomes in gamete-producing cells being reduced to one half and that involves a reduction division in which one of each pair of homologous chromosomes passes to each daughter cell followed by a mitotic division.

**MITOSIS** A process that takes place in the nucleus of a dividing cell, involves typically a series of steps consisting of prophase, metaphase, anaphase, and telophase, and results in the formation of two new nuclei each having the same number of chromosomes as the parent nucleus.

**MONOECIOUS** Relating to animals in which both sperm and eggs are produced by the same individual.

**MORPHOLOGICAL** Relating to or concerned with form or structure.

**MUTATION** An alteration in the genetic material (the genome) of a cell of a living organism or of a virus that is more or less permanent and that can be transmitted to the cell's or virus's descendants.

**NANOTECHNOLOGY** The art of manipulating materials on an atomic or molecular scale especially to build microscopic devices.

**PHENOTYPE** The observable characters of an organism resulting from the interaction of genotype and environment.

**PLASMID** A circular DNA molecule that originated from bacteria.

**PLURIPOTENT** Capable of differentiating into one of many cell types.

**PROPAGATE** To cause to continue or increase by natural reproduction; to have young or issue: multiply by sexual generation or by seeds, shoots, or cuttings.

**RECOMBINANT DNA** DNA prepared in the laboratory by breaking up and joining together DNA from several different species of organisms.

**REPRODUCTIVE CLONING** Cloning that involves the implantation of a cloned embryo into a real or an artificial uterus.

**SOMATIC CELL NUCLEAR TRANSFER (SCNT)** A technique in which the nucleus of a somatic cell is transferred to the cytoplasm of an enucleated egg.

**THERAPEUTIC CLONING** Cloning that is intended to use cloned embryos for the purpose of extracting stem cells from them, without ever implanting the embryos in a womb.

**XENOTRANSPLANTATION** The transplantation of animal tissues into humans.

**ZYGOTE** A one-celled embryo; a fertilized egg cell that results from the union of a female gamete with a male gamete.

An overview of the uses of cloning in molecular biology is Terry A. Brown, *Gene Cloning and DNA Analysis: An Introduction*, 6th ed. (2010). Nigel G. Halford, *Genetically Modified Crops* (2003), gives a historical account of genetic technology in the food industry, discusses the safety of genetically modified foods, and comments on the future of genetically modified crops. The role of genetics technologies in shaping livestock production is discussed in David L. Swain (ed.), *Redesigning Animal Agriculture: The Challenge of the 21st Century* (2007).

Introductions to reproduction in animals and animal breeding are D.S. Falconer and Trudy F.C. Mackay, *Introduction to Quantitative Genetics*, 4th ed. (1996); Richard M. Bourdon, *Understanding Animal Breeding*, 2nd ed. (2000); and Wilson G. Pond and Alan W. Bell (eds.), *Encyclopedia of Animal Science*, 2nd ed. (2011).

The science, applications, and philosophical issues of cloning are discussed in Glenn McGee (ed.), *The Human Cloning Debate*, 4th ed. (2004). The social, psychological, and ethical impacts of human cloning are discussed in Ian Wilmut and Roger Highfield, *After Dolly: The Uses and Misuses of Human Cloning* (2006).

Alan McHughen, *Pandora's Picnic Basket: The Potential and Hazards of Genetically Modified Foods* (2000), provides a skeptical perspective on the safety of genetically modified foods, focusing on the policies related to production and distribution of those foods.

John E.J. Rasko, Gabrielle O'Sullivan, and Rachel A. Ankeny, *The Ethics of Inheritable Genetic Modification: A Dividing Line?* (2006), explores the application of gene technology to human medicine and the ethical implications of human genetic modification. John C. Avise, *The Hope, Hype, and Reality of Genetic Engineering: Remarkable Stories from Agriculture, Industry, Medicine, and the Environment* (2004), covers a broad range of topics, from agriculture to medicine to bioterrorism, in remarkable detail and with reasonable objectivity. Issues related to the application of cloning and genetic engineering in conservation science are discussed in Markku Oksanen and Helena Siipi (eds.), *The Ethics of Animal Re-creation and Modification: Reviving, Rewilding, Restoring* (2014).